# Paris Postcards

Short stories by
GUY HIBBERT

VENTURA
EDITIONS

**PARIS POSTCARDS**

Copyright ©2020 by Guy Hibbert.

ISBN-13: 978-1986761024

ISBN-10: 1986761029

www.guyhibbert.com

This is a work of fiction. The characters and events described herein are imaginary and are not intended to refer to specific places or to living persons alive or dead. All rights reserved. No part of this publication may be reproduced, distributed, or transmitted in any form or by any means, including photocopying, recording, or other electronic or mechanical methods without the prior written permission of the publisher except for brief quotations embodied in critical reviews.

**Published by Ventura Editions, Cambridge House, BATH, BA1 1JS, UK.**

First edition, June 2018

VENTURA
EDITIONS

## A note from the author.

Walking the streets of Paris makes me feel an affinity with the past. I observe the foreign visitors drawn to such a magical city and among them all the residents going about their everyday lives. I think about people over the centuries whose footsteps I may be following, whether humble and long-forgotten citizens or those who had their moment of fame and made a small mark in history. What special place did the city hold in their hearts? What memorable moments took place here and what passions have been stirred, what loves lost or found?

Two things to note. Firstly, the stories in this book are written with different 'authorial' voices dependent on the time, place and character. Secondly, they are all linked to each other in some way through people or places. If you spot these links, I hope they make you smile and reflect on this sense of connectedness.

A note about the cover. The grand building in the distance behind the Eiffel tower is the Palais Trocadero, built in 1878 for the Exposition Universelle and destroyed in 1937 to make way for the Palais du Chaillot.

**CONTENTS**

Count Stanny ............................................................... 1

The Whip Hand ........................................................23

Resistance.................................................................49

Les Années Folles ....................................................79

Waiting...................................................................107

Russian Doll ...........................................................141

The Concierge.........................................................159

The Blue Dress ......................................................185

The Breath of Paris.................................................203

The Chemistry of Love...........................................223

Les Bouquinistes ........................................................1

# Count Stanny

## The Russian quarter, September 1925

I didn't realise at the time, but I was the only one who knew. It was only when Stanny left Paris that it truly dawned on me. I alone carried the burden of knowing his private history and I alone had been entrusted with passing the news on to Elodie and Maxim.

"André," he said, as he packed winter clothes into a large leather suitcase. "André, my friend, before I leave I have a special request of you. I ask you because I trust you and only you know my closest friends in Paris. Three days ago, I received news of Petrovich. He is alive. Because you know what happened to my family after the revolution, so you guess where it is I am going now. But never tell anyone, even Elodie."

He closed the lid of his case, took my hands firmly in his and looked at me with his deep, brooding eyes. "André, you don't know where I am going. I have just left. Vanished overnight. Yes? They have spies everywhere. Even the peasants are spies – you can trust no one. I will not be able to communicate with anyone here. Too dangerous. But listen, if I find him and my mission is successful I will send you a kind of coded message. Look at these two postcards André. If I send you the Eiffel Tower it means I have done it and I am on my way back. If I send you the Dôme des Invalides, it means I have done it, but I can never return. It may mean . . . well that doesn't matter. But you can be sure that I won't come back. Understood?"

I am ashamed to admit I felt a surge of pride. Stanny was like a father figure to us all and like a brother to me. He was a kind of everyday folk hero, and I, a grown man, felt at that moment, a foolish pride, like a schoolboy, that he had not only shared his terrible past with me but now I was honoured with this new secret commitment. But as the days passed and then the months with no word and I thought back on our time together I began to understand the truth of the perilous quest upon which he had embarked.

There was a time when we survivors were easy to recognise. The disabilities and ugly disfigurements. The medals polished and pinned to sky-blue uniforms for memorial ceremonies and valedictions. Do you know what they called me? 'Lucky André'. Four years serving France across five different fronts and nothing more than a broken arm and a dose of trench-foot to show for all my efforts to be killed in the name of my country. As the months and years passed we were patched up and dispatched home with our pensions and our medals, into the arms of wives and mothers who could never hope to understand. We had to try to begin again, to pick up some semblance of normal life, even though we felt the survivors guilt, living amidst the widows and orphans. Gradually, town centres once reduced to debris and rubble were bulldozed and re-built. Abandoned fields, livid with scarlet poppies, were farmed again. Trenches and fox-holes were filled and levelled, white bones and shell casings turned up in the wake of the plough. Caverns and shelters became overgrown with bramble and ivy. Memorials were erected, names carved and brass polished across the whole of Northern France: Verdun, the Somme, the Marne, the Alsace, the Ardennes.

Roll on four, five, six years and we've become almost invisible, because we are the living reminders of political and military folly, of millions who were loved and are now lost. But we're not invisible to each other. There's a sixth sense that we veterans have. That lanky figure at the bar, looking into the distance, blowing cigarette smoke out of the side of his mouth. I'll bet a hundred francs he's one. That bank manager with the streak of cruelty who won't lend a sou to help the farmers – he's one. That bearded, so-called poet, who hangs out in the Café du Palais drinking absinthe with all those arty types – you can be sure he's one. It's a look at the back of the eyes where the scars won't heal. It's disillusion, distrust, despair. It's masked pain and the dulling medicine of a repetitive job or strong alcohol. It's a yearning, a craving for release.

I know this because I've been there, tried all the remedies and treatments. Tried returning to the farm in Berry, to do what father would have expected. A hero's return. Embarrassing. *Fêtes champêtres*, bunting, bands and cakes. Not for me. Too many memories, too many open fields, endless earth and sky. A proper job at Uncle Fédéric's insurance firm in suburban Paris was next. Stuck it out for four years. Weighing, assessing, calculating risk. Shipwrecks, housefires, burglaries. Cocooned in paperwork and tedium, it worked for a while, the numbingly repetitive numbers, the structure of everyday work, the affable colleagues. But the evenings! Especially in the summer, the long light evenings and the insomnia. Another beer with the boys from work, getting drunk and behaving stupidly, upsetting the peacetime equilibrium. Apologising to Uncle: 'It won't happen again'. But it did. I wanted to upset things, I wanted to shout at the world, I wanted to fight again. Lucky?

Then in the late summer of '25 I met Stanny.

The Cloiserie de Lilas was packed. It wasn't my usual

hunting ground, too many pretentious types, but my flatmate François invited me; he'd always talked about the fun and the atmosphere and he said it would do me good. I suppose I was looking for something new. I'd been booted out of Uncle's business and now I needed something else to occupy my time, to distract my thoughts.

Extraordinary! From where did they emerge, all those painters and writers? Where were they in the War? North and South Americans, Eastern Europeans, Brits of course, even an Indian with a turban. We headed over to a lively group in a smoky corner where an animated, dramatic figure of a man, was holding court. He was mid-story, standing up with one foot on a chair, his hands sweeping the air as he illustrated some anecdote. There were about a dozen people gathered around he had them all enraptured. A young chap with floppy hair was sketching the scene, with big bold strokes of his charcoals.

"Meet the Count. The one and only Stanislaw Kerensky," said François.

It was quite a performance. A physically impressive man. Tall, broad shouldered. A regal bearing in the way he held his head and chin as he talked. Olive skinned with dark eyebrows and long wavy brown hair which touched the collar of an embroidered tunic. When he smiled he had a wide mouth under a noble moustache and you caught a glint from a gold tooth. But it was more the whole exuberant impression that was captivating, an aura. Women and men were equally enthralled.

We sat with the group. François introduced me but don't ask me to repeat all the names, except Kerensky of course. We drank beers, but I noticed the Russian was drinking champagne and vodka. When the opportunity arose I asked him, 'How long had he been in Paris?' It seemed a rather tame question, but he was surprisingly gracious in replying.

"Too long my friend. Since the Revolution. First Berlin, now Paris. I prefer Paris! Look at these beautiful people; such a wonderful city! It inspires me, this city."

"What does it inspire you to do?" I asked.

"To live, my friend, to live one day at a time, until I return."

"To Russia?"

"Of course. We will return and take back our mother country. It is just a question of time. And the small matter of a passport. But let's not spoil the evening with serious talk. I know a house where there will be a splendid party. You must come! François! Everybody listen! Who wants to see some Cossack dancing?!"

What followed later was just one night, one crazy madcap night in the company of the Count. Stanny they called him. There were many such nights, but I recall this one best

## COUNT STANNY

- as you do the first time you experience something truly unforgettable.

As soon as Stanny rose from his seat, downed his champagne, and picked up his hat, it was a cue for the whole crowd to stop their chatting and make quick decisions as to who was going to follow him.

He swept out of the Cloiserie, one arm around a very pretty girl, shouting something in Russian at the barman and tipping the doorman on the way out. François and I got into an old Peugeot with a couple of his friends and had to drive like idiots to keep up with Stanny in his huge Hispano-Suiza.

I said to François:

"My God, these people are pretty lively!"

"Just wait, you haven't seen anything yet."

"What's his story then?" I asked.

"White Russian. Prince or Count back in Belarus. Has money but no one's sure where it comes from. Seems to have a lot of contacts in the ministry. Came from Berlin and now he's the toast of Paris. All a bit of a mystery really."

"Pretty girls!" I shouted, over the engine noise.

"Russians mostly. Working as models and seamstresses. But there should be some French at the party too – don't worry!"

Racing around the Place des Ternes we followed the

sound of Stanny's roaring engine down a side street and into a large courtyard where he lurched to a halt and jumped out, followed by a couple of girlfriends teetering on their heels across the cobbled yard. Several other cars and taxis had managed to follow (all the taxis were driven by Russians in those days) and about ten of us followed Stanny up three flights of stairs. You could hear jazz music coming from somewhere above. Breathless, we all fell into the midst of a grand apartment where a crowd of rather exotic revellers were chatting, laughing and dancing.

It was as if our arrival heralded the start of the party proper. Everyone seemed to know Stanny and accepted us as if we were all part of the Count's personal entourage. As François went off to greet an old friend I lit a cigarette and took it all in. This would once have been a very fine apartment. Tall ceilings, plasterwork, a grand marble fireplace, a glittering chandelier. But it was well worn now. The plasterwork was cracked and broken, dust on the chandelier and frayed curtains at the windows. I liked it. It reflected how I felt. A woman in a shimmering, figure-hugging dress waved a white gloved hand and a cigarette holder and said, "Did you see La Bohème? Anastasia's costumes were divine."

The opera? Me? Evidently my conversation wasn't up to scratch because she soon left me alone, so I went in search of another drink. In the salon an old buffet was covered in bottles and ice buckets where I could see the necks of champagne bottles peeking out invitingly. As I filled a glass with bubbly a hand touched my arm and I recognised one of the girls from the Cloiserie.

"You look like you're French?" she said in a country accent I couldn't quite place. She introduced herself as Elodie. "Nothing against foreigners," she said, "but sometimes at these parties you can go a whole evening and not hear another word of French!"

"Don't you like the Russians?" I asked.

"Au contraire, I am Stanny's girlfriend, so I have no choice in the matter."

We chatted for a while about Paris, about bars and nightclubs. Although she was glamourous and pretty I could see she also had a shy charm which added to her allure. But there was no point me showing any interest - she was head over heels for Stanny and she told me about her new life in a kind of breathless outpouring.

"It's incredible how my world has changed since meeting this crowd. I used to have a very dull life and then I met Ludmilla . . .", she pointed out the auburn-haired beauty I recognised from the Cloiserie. "We became good pals and through her I met Stanny. He's quite the most extravagant man, you know. We've been to all the cabarets and music halls, the Alhambra, the Moulin Rouge, the little Lapin Agile and one time we saw Josephine Baker dance at the Champs-Elysées. Have you seen her? We sat right in the front row - she has amazing eyes. The atmosphere was electric – I've never heard or seen anything like her! I expect they'll be getting thirsty - let's go and join the fun!" she said as she picked up a bottle of champagne and gestured for me to follow.

We meandered through an odd assortment of merry-makers towards the source of the music and the loudest voices. Passing through some double doors I shall never forget the scene that appeared in front of my eyes: a whirling carousel of couples dancing the latest craze to some crackly jazz from a big old wind-up gramophone. Girls wearing low-backed narrow dresses flicking up their heels and twirling long necklaces as their partners attempted to keep up while clutching glasses and bottles of champagne. Among the bow ties and tuxedos, I noticed some of the men were wearing military uniforms – with a jolt I realised that these were the black and red tunics of White Russian officers. The whole spectacle was a crazy kaleidoscope of sound and colour set against the faded grandeur of gilt mirrors and parquet floors. But this was nothing compared to what was to follow.

An inconspicuous signal was the cue for all the Russians in uniform to form an inner circle within the crowd as an old greybeard veteran in the corner started to play a lively refrain on a battered fiddle. Immediately some of the uniformed officers started a rhythmic clapping while others took turns to link arms and stamp their leather boots in time to the music. It became a kind of manic competition, each one striving to outperform the previous, with greater feats of athletic dance and dramatic jumps and slapping of thighs. The crowd was cheering and clapping in a frenzy as Stanny and two other officers took to the centre of the ring and began that incredible Cossack dance where they squat down with their arms folded and kick out one leg then the other in perfect time to the beat of the music. What a spectacle! What strength in their legs and thighs! The whole room was in a kind of fervoured uproar as the three of them pushed themselves to the limit. The stamping and clapping shook the paintings on the walls and a fine dust drifted down from the old plaster ceilings and mouldings. In a show of bravado Stanny was handed a champagne saucer which he proceeded to drain with one hand while still kicking out his legs beneath him, and the other two were handed a tricolour flag which they waved over their heads. What a show! Eventually they all collapsed on each other, laughing and jostling and then Stanny jumped up and shouted "Bonne nuit! Poka! Levewohl! Arrivederci!"

And with that he picked up his fur hat and his coat and with Max, his drinking buddy, Ludmilla and Elodie in tow he headed for the door.

François gestured for us to follow so once again we found ourselves racing after Stanny's car, this time heading for the centre of Paris. By now my brain was becoming befuddled by the drink and the party atmosphere, but even so, my final memories of the evening remain vivid to this day. Stanny pushed the Hispano Suiza up to sixty or seventy on the Champs-Elysées and without slowing swung the big beast into a skidding turn around the cobbles of the Arc de Triomphe, heading back towards the river. François and I could hear the girls screaming and a few late-night strollers stared aghast at this lunatic display. We could hardly keep up but eventually we glimpsed them ahead making a turn towards the Eiffel Tower. We rounded the same bend and crossed the river just in time to see Stanny drive off the main road and race right underneath the tower itself. Then in a cloud of dust he whirled around again and back under the huge metal arches beeping the horn and waving madly at us as we arrived from the other direction, just as two gendarmes ran across his path and flagged him down.

"He's had it now," I said to François as we turned off our engine and tried to look nonchalant.

"Not necessarily," replied François. "Let's wait and see."

We watched as Stanny climbed out of the car and walked off with the agitated gendarmes, for all the world looking as if he would be hand-cuffed and taken to a cell. The girls looked worried. Max leaned against the bonnet, smoking. About five minutes later, we saw two figures returning. I have often recounted the story of what I saw that night – Stanny walking back towards the car with his arm around the shoulder of one of the gendarmes, chatting amiably as if they were comrades from years ago.

"Typical Stanny," said François. "He could wriggle out of anything."

People assumed it was like that all the time, that Stanny was always hosting a wild party or involved in some kind of scrape. But it wasn't so. I knew another side to him, thanks mainly to us both enjoying a game of chess.

He was visiting François one day at our shared apartment when he noticed the table and chess pieces set out.

"François, I didn't know you played the game of kings?"

"I don't. It's André who plays!" came a voice from the kitchen. "Ask him!"

We began playing regularly. He was a crafty player, patient, but sometimes lacking in concentration. But despite this we were well matched, and our games could last for days, picked up again on quiet Sunday mornings or winter evenings when other entertainments failed to catch Stanny's imagination.

It was during one such marathon session that we began

to compare game strategy, and this led on to talk of military campaigns. As Stanny spoke I noticed for the first time a look in his eye that I recognised, as if behind the radiance lay a sadness or a void. And I think he saw it in me as well. Late one evening we came to a stalemate in our game and I suggested a brandy to stimulate our tired minds.

"I like these times we spend playing chess," he said. "I find a kind of stillness within it. You have to focus on one thing only and all your thoughts about the game make you forget everything else."

"There's a kind of peace in it, isn't there?" I said.

"Yes, exactly. Ironic that a game based on war should create peaceful feelings." he replied.

"I suppose you are like me, you have things you need to forget?" I ventured.

"Many things," he said. "Many terrible things."

And to my surprise, after a pause, he began to speak in a solemn voice about the time before Berlin and Paris, about the years of the Revolution. As he spoke about his loyalty to the Czar, about the terrible sufferings of his comrades in arms, the bitter fighting through freezing winters, I could see his eyes burning with a cold flame. I refilled his brandy twice as he recounted the pain and frustration of having so little news of his family and the turmoil it caused him to see his country divided.

"Tell me about your family Stanny," I said, trying to be sympathetic.

He lit a cigarette and took another swig of brandy, and simply said, "All dead."

Before I could say more – in truth what could I have said – he carried on. "We returned to our village to find the Red Army had raised it to the ground. I had told my wife if the fighting came to our region to leave the manor house and take refuge in one of our old farmhouses in the valley. I thought they would be safe there. When I saw our beautiful house destroyed I began to fear the worst. I ran the whole way through the village and down to the valley. All my fears were confirmed, but worse, much worse. They had burned it to the ground. I found my wife, mother, my two girls and my son Vladimir, God bless them all, I found them in the charred ruins, all dead. Burned almost beyond recognition. Later I discovered that this was the handiwork, the hallmark of Red Army Commissar Petrovich. He cut a swathe of death and destruction through our region. That man is pure evil André, pure evil. I vowed then and there to have my revenge and by God I will."

What could I say? It was only because I recognised the anger and the pain that I felt justified in continuing to talk, brother to brother, to work through our grief-laden memories.

"In the army, they called me Lucky," I said. "Are we lucky Stanny? Lucky we survived? I have lost count of the friends I lost. Good friends, soul-mates you would die for, killed by gas or shell bursts or bullets. I've seen men drowning in the mud of fox-holes and you couldn't move an inch to help them because you choose to protect your own life, waiting for the cover of darkness. A boy was standing next to me in the trench, so young, and I told him how to protect his boots and where to piss and how not to move around, said I would keep an eye out for him, poor lad was only sixteen, and minutes, literally minutes later, he turned around to answer an instruction and lifted his head a fraction too high and a sniper took half his head off. He fell into my arms. I will never forget the look in his misting eyes that seemed to say: 'But I thought I was going to be alright if I just stuck with you?' So many, hundreds like that Stanny, hundreds, thousands, probably millions, and they called me Lucky. Tell me, are we lucky?"

We never spoke of it again. These memories are best left alone. Yet in those moments we forged an unexpected bond between us. We sensed the scars on our souls. Stanny pushed life to the boundaries, seeking adventure, danger, oblivion; anything to anaesthetize the memories. And I, well, after Stanny I remained restless and empty, hoping above hope that someone else or something else would fill the void and salve the pain. But my troubles and anxieties felt negligible when I remembered his tragic history. There was something magnificent and brave about his attitude to life. It was as if he too had been through that terrible fire. But like the flowers that lie buried after the forest fires have scorched the earth, so he had been able to flourish again once time had passed and the conditions were right. It was as if his journey had led him through a kind of sacred, redemptive fire of the mind. How else to comprehend his ability to savour life in all it's tragic glory? I didn't need to drink and attend all the parties or join in his crazy antics; just to know him and count him as a friend gave me back some sense of brief purpose to my life. In return it seemed to me I offered him time for quiet reflection, moments of peace and brotherly affection.

Alas, too short a time. Six months, and there we were on a freezing foggy February night, facing each other over his battered suitcase, and I was listening to his instructions like a dutiful disciple. And in my head, I was thinking, 'Is this just another mad adventure of Stanny's? Surely he will be back again soon?' But in my heart, I confess it was altogether another feeling. Fear, yes, real fear that I might never see him again. But something else too, I admit. I felt love, though perhaps at that time I would have dared not name it as such. But now, I look back on that time in Paris as one of the most memorable and momentous periods of my life. To have known Maxim, Elodie, Ludmilla and François had been a joy and a privilege. To have known, to have been a true friend and confidante of Stanny's, and to have shared a brief part of the extraordinary world of Count Stanislaw Kerensky had been an honour and a gift.

After he left I kept my word. 'Vanished into the night,' I repeated. 'Probably back to Russia,' we all said to ourselves, 'back to find his family or his money.' We were flat. Life was flat. Friends drifted apart. Parties were never the same. The chess pieces gathered dust. Elodie, poor Elodie, was distraught, phoning us and calling by in search of news, badgering some of Stanny's old gang in search of clues. But the trail was cold and as time passed our ordinary lives demanded our attentions. We began to talk nostalgically of Stanny, he began to blend inexorably into the pool of our other memories - only his memory burned the brightest and best of them all. It was Elodie who kept an eternal torch lit for Stanny. She had discovered soon after he left Paris that she was expecting his baby. If she could only tell him this precious news, she felt sure in her heart that he would return one day.

In the late summer of '26 I began to think of returning to the farm. For the first time I felt a surprising lightness of heart as I pictured its rolling fields. One evening in Paris we saw a huge golden moon rise behind the Palais and it put me in mind of the hills and lakes of Berry, fishing as a boy in slow moving river waters and picking plums and apples from the orchard. As harvest time approached it was with some trepidation that I visited the cousins and, although the farm was in my name, I asked them as diplomatically as possible if my return to those pastures would be welcomed. I stayed for a blissful week, bending my back to whatever task they threw at me, and taking hot baths at night to soothe my aching muscles.

On returning to Paris it was in this gratifyingly refreshed state of mind that I returned to my new apartment, collected the post that had gathered in the box since my departure, and sat down with a coffee to sift through the bills and other tedious correspondence. There, nestled between two large envelopes, was a postcard with a Russian stamp, addressed to me.

I hadn't forgotten of course. It's just that sufficient time had passed for other thoughts and plans to have occupied my mind and for that reason I did not initially jump out of my chair, but looked with curiosity at the strange message which said:

*Leningrad much improved since the Revolution. Very satisfactory visit. Ever your friend. S.*

Well then it all came flooding back to me, and I can't

begin to describe the sickness I felt in the pit of my stomach before turning the card over. How could such a small insignificant thing be the catalyst of such emotion? On the other side of the card was the Dôme des Invalides. There were no other words or clues. Nothing else around which to construct a theory or start a rumour, no grounds for hopeful speculation. The Dôme des Invalides – Napoleon's tomb. It was typical of Stanny to tease out a nugget of black humour from the script of a heart-rending drama.

I kept putting it off – telling the others, especially Elodie, who was nursing her baby Sergei. But it had to be done, so later that week I invited François, Ludmilla and Elodie to my apartment where they sat looking expectantly at me. I opened a bottle of vodka and insisted they drink a few glasses before I told them the news. I said simply, "I have some very limited but very definitive news about Stanny."

As one, they gasped and stared in astonishment at me. Elodie put both hands to her cheeks in shock.

"I am sorry I can't tell you anything much, but I do know for certain he is not going to return to Paris. I also know that he loves you all, especially you dear Elodie."

They pressed me on it, but I had sworn a vow to Stanny. Anyway, what would it have served to tell them what I knew? They all suspected he was involved in a spying game or some dangerous Monarchist insurrection. I said to myself, 'They just need time to come to terms with his disappearance'. It marked the end of something. We all needed to move on, perhaps for good.

With François promising to take care of Elodie and the baby in Paris, I felt increasingly drawn back to the calm of the countryside. Autumn found me back on the farm again, helping with the final harvest and preparing for winter. It was pleasingly predictable work, and I was surprised to find solace in the beauty of the seasons. That winter I met Emilie, a local girl, I hate to say not as pretty as the Russian princesses I had known, but wholesome and good-hearted enough to take me on, damaged goods as I surely was, and we married not long after. In the winter evenings, when it was too dark to tend the farm, we would sit by the fire in the old farmhouse kitchen and by the glowing candlelight I began to read the great Russian writers; Dostoyevsky, Gogol and Chekhov. One such evening, Emilie, who was expecting our baby at the time, leaned over and took from within the pages of my novel the bookmark I used.

"What is this postcard? The Dôme des Invalides, Napoleons' tomb? Rather gloomy isn't it. But I notice you always use it."

"Yes, you're right my darling. It is important to me. It reminds me of Paris, a time and a place that was very special to me."

And then I added, almost as an afterthought, "And of someone I knew and loved, someone who, now I think about it, made me realise something about myself."

"And what is that my sweet?" Emilie said with a raised eyebrow.

I took her hand and said, "That I am lucky".

# The Whip Hand

## 16th Arrondissement, January 1937

I run the back of my hand through the gowns that hang in the armoire – it is comforting to feel the rippling touch of silks, satins, brocades, chiffons and velvets, feathers and plumes. 'How do I feel?' I wonder.

Not sad exactly or homesick. Some days the melancholy feeling just comes unbidden, like a late frost that arrives to spoil a cherry-blossomed day in our beloved Passy.

But today, of all days, before the party at Hermione Morisot's. What poor timing! Now I will have to try and build myself up on my own. The usual set will turn out and Hector will expect me to shine. "Alice, s'il te plait, run me a hot bath and put in that new scented oil from Le Bon Marché."

I slick my hands down my still freckled arms and admire my legs glistening in the oily water. These legs look indulged - only a decade ago they were muscled and bruised from ranch-work, now they're as fine and sleek as a filly at

Longchamp. The hot water and the aromas are soothing.

What to wear? There'll be Hermione's usual mixed crowd…it's her gift to mingle and blend in different sets. She could flirt with a poet, talk money with the bankers, tease an old aristocrat and still have enough charm on tap to tickle the dullest politician. How does she do it?

Dare I show off the peach Balenciaga? No, it's too revealing, and I don't feel like the attention tonight. The black lace Chanel? Too sombre? What would Hector like me in? Something striking but classic…the white bias Schiaparelli with the fuchsia satin?

Alice curls my hair as I put on my make-up, then carefully match my nail varnish to my coral lipstick. What a performance this has become. It's a far cry from the old morning routine. A quick flannel wash in cold water and a firm brush through my hair – seems like it was thicker and golder back then - before throwing on dungarees and a checkered shirt, fit and fresh-faced and ready for the day. Ten years ago, was it, or eleven? They wouldn't recognise me now, but under all this the glamour I know there's more than a trace of Texas dust.

I arrive at Hermione's early – *quel faux pas!* Why couldn't he leave his business on time for once and accompany me! What was it he had said, some kind of import or shipment of grain delayed? Or was it beef? One of his winner-takes-it-all schemes no doubt. The traffic was light, and the car had arrived too soon. Of course, I should have told Stéphane to take another tour around the block, but never mind, *tant pis*, here I am. Fortified with a chilled Mary Pickford and a deeply inhaled Sobranie I meander around the salon with time to admire Hermione's new decor.

Pale walls in creams and greys, but that extraordinary wall-painting like a jungle scene from Malaya or India. What would you call that, a mural? A trompe-l'oeil? The black onyx panthers either side of that wonderful Empire fireplace How on earth does she put these gorgeous things together? An inlaid walnut table with the huge vase of gold or gilded lilies – is that real gold or just paint? A chromium legged table on an Aubusson rug! Family portraits (are they really family or just bought in some auction like the ones Hector pretended were his ancestral hand-me-downs?). And then some kind of hideous modern mess of daubed paint over here - probably all the rage in Berlin or Vienna. Hector will know who we can get to fix up our place, it seems so stodgy and staid compared to this. But Hector does love his grand baronial style. Would he ever let a modernist decorator loose on the house in Passy?

Looking down from the tall window there are cars drawing up outside the town-house, doors are opening and soon they will all make their colourful entrances. I am silently berating myself for my premature entrance when there's an unmistakeable whooping in my ear.

"Darling Daisy, my absolute *favourite* American in Paris! Don't stand all on your lonesome dear, come and meet Salomé and Django – I am too, too lucky to persuade them to entertain us tonight!"

It's Hermione, and she is ravishing as usual, wearing a sapphire silk number, almost certainly Chanel. She wafts across the salon with me in tow, as a maid opens the huge panelled doors into a heavily gilded ball-room and across a polished chestnut floor to where are gathered two or three musicians surrounded by guitars and African drums.

I catch my breath. Surely not Django Reinhardt? That night at the Grosse Pomme was unforgettable. Jazz but with guitars and violin and that incredible black singer. But it's him for sure, the dapper gypsy guitarist.

"Django, let me introduce you to a famous American beauty - Daisy Ignacio de Carrera."

"Enchanté, mademoiselle," he whispers, taking my hand in his and planting a little kiss.

"Oh Daisy ignore all that Mademoiselle nonsense, he's such a flirt!" says Hermione and then in a teasing manner she wags her finger at Django. "Now Monsieur Reinhardt, you'd better be a good garcon because Daisy's a happily married lady."

He's suave and charismatic, for sure. But also, kind of enigmatic. From another door emerges a lithe black woman in a stunning crinkled silver dress. What is that fabric? It's like she's wrapped in aluminium foil. I want to meet her, but Reinhardt seems a little fidgety to get back to his band, so I make an excuse and head back to the salon.

Now they make their entrances. The 'darlings' and 'divines', the 'mon cheries' and 'my dears', the sigh of silk scarves and shawls as they are cast off to reveal the latest couture creations, the rustle and sheen of money. There's Marie-Louise de Bernaccio, married three times and now said to have an eye for the Prince of Wales. Some chance! Never noticed how her teeth are so white. She's wearing a gaudy necklace of ruby droplets and what look like tiger teeth. Animal designs are de rigueur in the set these days.

The volume of chatter increases, and I wonder: should I wait for them to come my way or head on over? Why don't I know what to do? My instincts don't work well here. I have instincts; for a pony with a wild streak, for the smell of an early summer storm across the savannah – some help they are now.

There's Edmond Gracy in a strange corduroy suit and a silk cravat and he's with a woman I don't recognise, another little muse he's acquired along the way I guess. Tried it that time with me, said I was his American 'Ice Diamond' or some such nonsense, anyway his arrows missed me by a mile. Does he invite himself to these parties or is he part of the entertainment? There'd be others soon in the arty set, probably that Stein woman and a Spanish artist or two. At least they paint like real artists - the rest of them are busy trying to make their spoiled lives into a work of art.

A voice with a Southern drawl says, "Oh my dear God, it's Daisy McManners. I do declare it really is you!", and I'm panicking for a moment because I know this tall thin man but not here. He belongs somewhere else in my past, not in the Paris part of my brain.

"You look utterly ravishing my dearest Daisy - I never thought to meet you here!" he says, holding my hand in a brotherly kind of way.

Well, darn me, if it isn't Frank Fonseca!

"Frank, I can't believe it! It was New York, what five years ago?"

We do that thing you do in these situations, 'You look so well! What brings you to Paris' and so on. And I'm half listening to what he is saying because at the same time another part of my mind is trying my darndest to recall how far it went with him and whether he knows about the inheritance and about Hector and Paris. But then, does it matter anyway? I mean, Frank was always just like a friend, a brother, for the most part anyway. He's wearing a very straight suit with a snazzy little bow-tie. Just a little nod towards fashion, good old Frank. And then sotto voce he says "You'll never guess! Diana Vreeland's taken me on to write for Harpers! I just got here about three weeks ago. Came in on the Normandie, fabulous ship. My god Daisy, you look a million dollars! Where's that gauche girl I used to know!"

More cocktails and reminiscing, then the band starts up and instantly it's like liquid sunshine pouring into the salon and everyone is smiling and laughing. Reinhardt's got a second guitarist with him and the other guy has this wicked rhythm going as Django does his thing, fingers zipping along the fretboard, just as it was that night at the club. That's their name; the Hot Club de France. Now the girl, Salomé, she's singing some kind of counterpoint to his guitar and everyone turns and applauds her first few verses and then we're back to it. This is what we do. We live like kings and princes, we party like Maharajas, like we were born to it. But we weren't born to it. At least not me. And not Claudette Bonbois over there either. I know for a fact she was brought up in a poor mill family in Belgium. But with a body like hers, (and no qualms about sharing it around they say), she's even adorned the cover of Vogue. Meanwhile Frank has gone to hunt for more cocktails. How far do I want to go down memory lane with him? Where the hell is Hector anyway? Speaking of Maharajas, there's a real live one in the corner with poor Nancy Cunard, she's buttonholing him, probably asking him to take sides in the Spanish Civil War. I heard she's publishing again.

Frank hands me a glass and I whisper, "Frank, that fabulous gentleman in the corner is the Maharaja of Kapurthala. Look at that turban with the emerald! They say he supplies most of the precious stones for Cartier."

I drink too quickly. Frank lights a cigarette for me. He has come on a bit, looks easier in his own skin. Speaks confidently. But still you can tell he's new to this world. He's still bright eyed and bushy tailed off the boat from Manhattan. Too eager. Salomé is hitting some big notes now and the atmosphere is electric. Hermione weaves her way around the room, the ultimate hostess, gracious, charming, witty, knowledgeable. She's exotic, like a hothouse orchid. I wish I wasn't called Daisy. Too late to change I guess.

There's a commotion over at the main door. Everyone continues their conversation, but heads and eyes can't help turning. This must be Hector. Who else would arrive with such theatricality and an entourage in tow. He must have collected them on his way here. There are the Coopers and Emilio Terry and, oh no he hasn't! He has, he's brought Fernando and that means one thing only. They've stopped at the Cuba Bar on their way. No wonder he's roaring in.

Hector Ignacio de Carrera. How would you describe this

man, my husband? What would a rookie journalist like Frank make of Hector? Warm, earthy? Passionate, fiery? Cavalier, impulsive? All these things and more. A man's man for sure: a cigar smoking, polo-playing, hunting, shooting, hard drinking caballero. And yet, also, a woman's man: a man attractive to other women, a man with confidence in his warm blood, a figure of command, a man capable of chivalry and charm. No wonder they adored him, the men and the women, and even those still undecided on their final gender.

Shouts of "Don Hector!" from across the room as he makes his way towards me, kissing hands and slapping backs left and right, picking up a glass of champagne with one hand and throwing his scarf over a chair with the other. Reminds me of our first meeting in New York. Suddenly the atmosphere in the room crackles as conversations pause momentarily, and his friends shout endearments and those who want to be his friends wave and try to catch his eye.

Hector stops in front of me and produces an elaborate bow. It's ironic, he's playing to an audience, but still he charms me.

"My darling, a thousand apologies for my late arrival, you look absolutely radiant. You obviously haven't missed me!"

We kiss, and he squeezes my arm and then lets his hand

brush down the side of my satin dress and rest on my hip. I know what's he's doing. It's his way of saying to everyone 'She's mine'. To the men in the room he's saying, 'You can only dream of her naked, but I possess her entirely' and to the women 'I am a big hunter – see my bounty. Imagine what I could do for you'.

I know this to be true. How do I feel about it? I think I hate, no I *do* hate being displayed like a prized chattel. It makes me feel like an adornment, part of the latest decor in the set of Hector's splendidly staged life. And yet, is it not also exciting and thrilling, to be revered and envied, to be treated to any bauble or trinket on a whim, to be indulged and even to be possessed? For all the society induction in New York, the finishing school in Montreux, for all the language lessons and trips to Florence and Rome, still I'm a keen-eyed Texas range girl underneath all this finery. I was brought up around big strong men who took decisions and never feared to speak their minds.

We're in a group now, with Louisa de Foulonger, who hosts delightful candlelit soirées at the Chateau Chabrol (but whose English is endearingly comical); Charlie "Chatty" Musgrove who apparently owns half of Belgravia and a couple I haven't seen before who seem to know Hector. Louisa introduces them. "Daisy, do you know the Lafarges? Chantelle and Fédéric, they just opened the

Normandie? Have you been? It's divine! Mouth-watering menu and the interior is all done in the most fabulous beaux-arts style you can imagine!"

Do I care what they are all talking about? Society gossip: some impresario has upset the latest Russian émigré ballerina, or Max von Someone, the German film director is a closet Nazi or else it's innuendos about a royal princess and her infatuation with the Duke of Navarra or somewhere in Spain. What is that bon-mot they all recite? 'Never be afraid to be vulgar, just boring'. I suspect I am boring. Hector offers me a cigarette and lights it for me - it's an intimate gesture as he touches my hand with his finger, while laughing and smiling at a long-winded story Charlie is telling.

You can feel the pulse of the room quicken. The band plays what they are calling gypsy jazz, and Django does look just like a suave, moustachioed, tuxedoed gypsy. The music has a languorous but insidious rhythm, it's offbeat tones blend with Salomé's voice as it swirls around the salon, breaking in and out of conversations. It matches my mood, it's mellow, the way three cocktails make you mellow, but it's also kind of mournful or reflective and that connects with me too, but I can't think why.

Frank circles in on me again. I introduce him to Hector, wondering if there might be an awkwardness. I mean, here's this young man from my life before Hector. We nearly had a thing me and Frank and a scene flashes into my memory, an apartment in Manhattan, a few too many martinis and a long embrace in a taxi with snow on the ground in Central Park. But that was it. There could have been more. Should have been more? But Hector isn't fazed one iota, he's chutzpah personified.

"I only wish I had your luck to have known Daisy as a girl. She must have been pure delight" he says to Frank with a kind of roguish glint in his eye.

"She was, still is a delight, and you're a lucky man!" retorts Frank and then he says to Hector "May I borrow your wife for five minutes? I have some old talk of New York chums I'd like to share with her and I fear it would only bore you."

We meander through the throng looking for a quiet corner. I pause to have a word with Countess Maria. It's hard to believe she came from Russia nearly twenty years ago – her face betrays her age of course, but her style! She still runs the last of the great fashion houses and I complement her on the most sensational outfit – a classic flowing gown in iridescent blue decorated with peacock feather hand printed motifs and an organza collar. Only she could carry it off.

Frank passes me a bubbling, fizzing cocktail, Chartreuse green this time, and pulls me conspiratorially into a corner.

"Listen", he says "I need your help. I'm here on a provisional trial. If I don't file some juicy stories for the magazine, Diana's not going to extend my contract. So how about helping out an old pal?"

An old pal, is that what we are now, old pals? And what do I owe him anyway?

"Frank, you've got the wrong girl if it's gossip you want."

"Not gossip," he says, "I need society stories, you know, who's making the news with art or fashion or making a million out of some thrilling investment."

I take a drag on my cigarette and my head begins to swirl a little. I'm looking at the abstract painting and I notice what might be a breaking wave only it's too green. Maybe it's a fern blowing in the wind? The decor suddenly makes sense, its clashing tones and eclectic mixtures belong to these times, to these people, to this music.

"You should talk to Hermione, she's the hostess with the mostest. I'm just the tinsel on the tree." I say to Frank, quite pleased with my wit.

"Why not something about you, doll?" he says. "Your story has got everything: hard knock Texas childhood, oil-boom millionaire heiress meets Chilean aristocrat, lives glamourous life of the rich and famous."

"Is that really how you see it?" I ask Frank.

"That's how our readers want to hear it...whether that's

the truth is another matter honey!"

"I don't know Frank, maybe. Let me talk to Hector. What would it involve?"

"What would it involve? Well, for starters, being interviewed by a fine sympathetic writer like me; followed by a flattering photo session, probably modelling some fancy couture and who knows maybe we can even tease Beaton away from Vogue . . . a backdrop of some country chateaux maybe, or your place if you prefer?"

What do I prefer? I don't prefer at all. 'No' is what I'm thinking. Frank has gotten too pushy since I last knew him. But then again Hector would probably love it because it would make him more famous and he'd see it is a good profile-raising business investment - get him some new connections. And would I secretly love it too? Isn't that my story? So why hide away from the reality?

"Frank sweetheart, I'm going to the little girl's room, so scram and see who else you can lure into your sordid publishing world!"

I edge out of the salon into the hall and the music and the din begins to recede. Old Madame Durane, the mother of the Foreign Secretary, is sitting on a chaise peering into her handbag looking intently for something. I should greet her, but she is distracted, and I glide by. The truth is I need fresh air, or maybe to sit calmly for a few minutes. Feeling a little too confident thanks to the alcohol (what do they put in these cocktails?), I dare to head up the marble stairs in search of a quiet place and at the top I turn into a corridor. I'll say I'm looking for a powder room. I open several doors. A cupboard, a bedroom, a dressing room. Hermione's dressing room? I enter and quietly close the door behind me. I walk to the window, open it a fraction and breathe in the winter air - a cool caress on my forehead and cheeks. I sit on an upholstered window-seat and move my shoulders forward and back to relieve some tension. Why am I tense?

This gets me thinking. When was the last time I was truly relaxed, truly myself? My real self? Certainly not in the ballrooms and salons of Paris. Is that me with Hector when we make love? Am I really there? He is so passionate, so fiery and animalistic that he carries me with him and he gives me pleasure I haven't known before. But sometimes I feel I am looking down at us, at myself, like I'm watching a scene on a stage.

The ranch in Hill Country seems such an eternity ago, yet only ten years. I picture myself aged seventeen, blue jeans and pink check work shirt, sweet on Luke Miller, the hired ranch-hand, pinching my cheeks to put a little glow on them before I go to help out. Riding like the wind across the grassland plateau, taking the horses to water in Willow Creek, or just sitting out on the porch with Grannie's lemonade or a Coca-Cola, the bottle chilled in the shiny new refrigerator. And then way before that time, before we had the money and the big ranch, I remember Pop and Uncle Jake, wildcat prospectors, coming home one night to say they had struck the motherlode – oil, oil, oil – dirty black gushers! All that graft and dusty work turning into millions and millions of dollars, which turned year by year into education and proper betterment for the family and buying a bigger ranch and a place on the Galveston coast, then New York and Switzerland for me. But no Mom or Pop to enjoy it anymore. Just millions and millions turning my world upside down, turning me into, into what?

On Hermione's peach glass dressing table are exquisitely moulded perfume bottles: Roger & Gallet, Lentheric. I lift the caps and inhale the heady scents of jasmine, orange, musk, rose. There are lipsticks in different shades, powder cases, cold cream, pearl and jade earrings and an amber necklace. These bijoux have been tried and hastily discarded. She must have hurried to finish her make-up, so she could come and greet me. A deep drawer is left slightly open. Shocked at my own audacity, I lean over and slide it open. What might I discover about the queen of café society?

At the back of the drawer are letters and postcards tied with ribbon. I look over at the dressing room door, to make sure it is closed tight, then quickly untie the ribbon. It's a little disappointing. There are letters from Wallace,

Hermione's husband, currently in South Africa, and many letters and postcards from relatives and friends I don't know. But wait a minute. I recognise this handwriting on the back of a postcard of the SS Queen Mary. My heart skips a beat as I stare at the long looping lines of Hector's unmistakeable script.

'Chère Hermione, am finally enjoying a long, lustful, laugh-filled love at sea. Mais oui, I am all at sea! Does Paris miss me? Of course not! Yours con gran admiracion x H.'

The date is June 1937. That's only six months ago! When was he on the Queen Mary? And what love at sea? Then another, from Santiago, in September.

'Chère H. Springtime in my home city! You would love the air that comes from the mountains (still with snow!), but the parties are nothing compared to yours. Luckily W is by my side and is a true companero anomarado. (Yes, this is a special one!) Yours con gran etc'

Shocked, I quickly fold the card and hide it in my purse. In a kind of trance, I put the cards and letters back, carefully tied with the ribbon, and slide the drawer shut. I close the window and ease the dressing room door open an inch to see if anyone is coming.

I feel unsteady on my feet, holding tightly to the handrail as I descend the stairs. A maid shows me to the ladies' room. I lock the door and stare blindly at my reflection in the mirror. What do I see? What would you see? You would see my golden wavy hair, cut and teased by the finest coiffeuse on the Rue de Rivoli into a swirling confection that frames the fair, many would say beautiful, green-eyed, oval face of a tall, blonde woman in her late twenties, wearing a very expensive white and pink party gown. You would see a diamond necklace and matching earrings that whisper the word "Cartier", a Tiffany cocktail watch and a discreet but elegant selection of rings containing rare gemstones sourced by a certain Maharaja before being painstakingly polished by the best Russian Jewish goldsmiths into glittering bands that grace long elegant fingers with French manicured nails.

And what do I see? I see a phoney. I see a pining creature in a gilded cage. A simple songbird painted up to resemble a bird of paradise, suitable for the display cabinet of a bigtime hunter or a collector of beautiful things. I see an awkward, naïve girl dressed like a princess. I see a fool, a dupe. I see I am bought and sold as much as any bijou on the Place Vendôme. I see a woman who has learned everything in her new role by soul-numbing practice and in doing so has lost her natural self.

I can't stand here all night. But without any kind of plan, and my head still spinning, I leave the powder room and head like a ghost back towards the raging din of the salon.

What will await me? Will I make a scene? Or play the ice-queen? Keep my card (my postcard!) close to my chest? But what would it all mean anyway? What would I do and where would I go? Back to a ranch in West Texas?

A hand grasps my elbow. I look around. It is Eveline Durane.

"Shall we take a turn my dear? You look a little pale. Perhaps a stroll in the conservatory? I do so hate the cacophony of these parties."

Dearest Madame Durane! Like a resilient Edwardian aunt amid the whirligig of the modern world, always a word of sound advice or a note of common sense.

"My dear," she says, "You must tell me what the matter is!"

I try to wriggle out of it and pretend I have just felt a little feint, probably too many cocktails (and that part is true). But she insists. "I haven't been on this planet for seventy years without learning to recognise an inner turmoil when I see one! We have got to know each other a little over the last year have we not? Come and sit here and talk to Madame Eveline."

And the extraordinary thing is . . . I do talk to her. And then to my embarrassment I can't help spilling it all out. In a long rambling outpouring of frustration and doubt and fear and uncertainty I tell her that I wonder in truth who I am and what am I doing here and whether I will ever fit in with these people and how they are all so fascinating and full of personality and how I feel plain and inconsequential and how I love Hector and he I think loves me but then what is love and now as I have always suspected but wanted to ignore it seems he sees other women and what does that make me and what on earth, what on earth am I to do!?

I lean forward and let my head fall against the soft brocade of her ample lap and cry like a child, and Madame Eveline Durane, matriarch of one of the most noble and influential families of France, places her hand on my head and gently runs her fingers through the waves of my hair.

"Such soft blonde locks you have. And my family is all so dark or grey like me," she says.

For a few moments I am a child back in the kitchen of the wooden house I grew up in and I have cut my finger or burnt my hand and I'm feeling the pain and the injustice of it. I'm sitting on Mama's lap and she is rocking me and saying special words that only she knows can make the pain go away and the world a better place again.

Madame Durane speaks softly to me, "Listen my dearest Daisy, in time you will see that none of this matters as much as you imagine, and your emotions are getting the better of you. Now do what I always do at times such as this and count your blessings. Shall I start it off? Let me see, how does it go? Something like this perhaps? I am young and beautiful. I am still young enough to have children. I have nearly all my adult life ahead of me. I live in Paris, the home of the most wonderful art and culture, the envy of other capital cities. I am married to a charming handsome man who has many friends and a great spirit of adventure. I have inherited more money than a thousand ordinary men will make in their lifetime. And when I awake every day in my fine apartment all I have to do is to decide how to entertain myself. Now I ask you Daisy, does this sound like a life that any sane person would find remotely upsetting?"

She has a clever, knowing way with words. The way she says it makes me laugh, laugh at her words and at myself. I sit up and dab my eyes with a hankie. "But what about Hector," I say, "and I miss my old life too."

"I've got news for you my dear," she says. "Firstly, I know Hector of old, I've seen him when he was first in Paris, a typical South American dowry hunter. I thought him uncouth and pompous, not a very winning combination. But I have to say he has changed for the better, he has a warm heart and his friends are loyal to him even when his schemes backfire, and that is always a good sign. But a man like Hector will never be a conventional husband. You take away that zest for life and he will lose his fire and soul. He would be like, like a trapped tiger. Let him have his freedom. Let him have a long leash. He loves you, but he will stop loving you if you try to tame him or challenge him. And besides, if he ever goes too far, well you have the whip hand. 'The whip hand', isn't that what you would say back on your ranch in Texas?"

"Why do I have the whip hand?"

"Because you have all the money, Daisy."

"But Hector has money too," I reply.

"Hector's money is a mystery to us all. They say it ebbs and flows like the tide, depending on the prospects of his latest deal. One thing is for sure, you can only truly count on Hector's money when you see a big pile of it sitting right in front of you. What he has in real cash is nothing compared to you. So, speak to your banker and when Hector misbehaves too much have your man cut off the supply."

"And as for Texas," she continues, "well what's to stop you going back more often? You have the means, just tell Hector that's the way it is. He has his escapades and all you ask is to be free to visit your homeland, to recharge your soul."

I see the ranch-house in my mind, all spruced up with every picket fence freshly whitewashed and all the post and rails neatly mended and a dozen strong horses running in the paddocks. And Uncle Jake at the head of the table with a fine Sunday suit and the cousins in their pretty frocks (and they will be fifteen or more now!) and I know it's what I need most. I must go there.

"Thank you, Eveline, thank you. I am so sorry to have blubbed like a silly girl. I guess this has all just been boiling up in my head for some time. I'm so glad we spoke, you won't tell anyone will you? I need to think things over, but I see the sense of your advice. It's just, I've been such a fool really, not to see the truth of my situation."

And she holds my hand again and stares directly into my eyes as I stand and prepare myself for, for what? To re-enter the salon of my past, or is it the salon of my future?

"Now don't do anything foolish that you might come to regret will you?" she says still holding both my hands. "Act in haste and you'll repent at leisure, and remember dear, to count those blessings."

I bend down and kiss her on both cheeks and walk out of the conservatory towards the salon and the whirlwind of music and laughter. How her words ring in my ears, like something dear Mama would have said, pure and true, they give me a simple courage.

I push my shoulders back and with a forced smile I return to the party maelstrom. What am I going to do now? Frank is across the room and he catches my eye, but no, I'm not going there, that's the soft option. Where's Hector? I'm not chickening out of this. I want to look him in the eyes.

He's walking into the ballroom with Hermione on his arm and Fernando is with him too, and that obsequious little yes-man, Joseph Adler, is creeping along behind trying to get into their conversation.

I join them but before I can get in any kind of salvo at Hector (not that I have anything prepared), he turns and spreads his arms wide towards me. "Chérie, where have you been? I was going to send a search party for you!" and instantly his arms wrap me up and he squeezes me the way he does. And Hermione winks knowingly at me - so disarming, is it a conspiratorial wink? Is she telling me she knows something I don't know? Or she knows that I know?

Then Hector points me to the band and says, "Daisy, look who is here! It's only that magician Reinhardt that we saw at the club." And to Hermione, "What little tricks did you pull to get him here, you are fiendishly persuasive Madame H!"

Why did I imagine Hector would look different now in my eyes? Did I really expect to re-join the party and see a pair of horns on his head? I can't say anything here and now, can I? How callow and petty that would seem. What to do? Take a deep breath. Count my blessings? Guests are on the dance floor now. The tune is jaunty yet sad, infectious. Salomé's voice has echoes of hope and yearning. There's only one thing to do. I turn to Hector and look into his eyes and for a split second I catch in his look some flicker of realisation, some acknowledgement of a change, a tiny question mark, or am I imagining it?

"Dance with me," I say.

He's a very good dancer. He has natural Latin rhythm, can do the rumba and tango better than most. But tonight it's all swing style and Lindy hop (if you can do it) and jitterbug and everyone is moving quickly to the jazz and you're caught up in a rush of whirling arms and legs and the heady scent of a dozen perfumes. Above me a glittering chandelier seems to careen out of control and for a second as we spin I catch our reflection in a huge gilded mirror.

What I glimpse is myself, Daisy McManners, the girl from a dust-bowl outback, starring in a kind of dazzling scene from a movie, like Ginger Rogers in 'Top Hat'. Yes, it's little old me, dressed like a princess, being whirled around by a handsome South American against a kaleidoscope of beautiful, happy people.

And I try to think about my situation, but I'm dizzy and it's hard to know what to feel. I just look into Hector's eyes. At each turn and twist he holds my gaze, unashamed, loving. I'm looking as hard as I can, I'm looking like I used to look into the soulful eyes of wild mustangs to see into their minds and try to divine if they were truly tamed. But I can't see it, just can't see it – there's no guile in these eyes, there's no deceit. All I see is insouciance. Hector is just what he is and what he always will be. An adventurer, a lover, an old-style gentleman, a buccaneer, a romantic, a charmer. And how can I not love him for himself?

On the way home, I lie in his arms in the back of the car, thinking. And I vow to myself that one day I will have my moment. Maybe not tonight or tomorrow. Probably not even this year. I will give Frank his magazine story and Hector will adore me for it. I will see the bank and get a grip on the money. I will go back to Texas for a vacation. I will buy myself another necklace or another horse. I will play Daisy Ignacio de Carrera. But one day, one day for sure, maybe even when we are grey and old, I will have my moment with Hector and until then he will not know what I know. I will wait until the time is right. I will wait until the price is right. And that may not seem like much but until that day I will hold this precious knowledge close to my heart, knowing that in some strange way it gives me the power to be true to myself, and that feels more precious than anything money can buy in this life.

*Resistance*

## Occupied Paris, November 1943

Lucienne woke with a start in her small bedroom at the top of the house on Rue Samarande in the early hours. It was a Friday night and the soldiers had been out to the clubs and brothels. They came carousing into the house, slamming doors and making futile attempts to walk quietly across the wooden floors. She heard Abelard, Oberstleutnant Neumann, open his door on the floor below her and bark at them to behave and shut up.

Her bedroom window in the attic was blacked out by a blind but still a sliver of silvery moonlight crept in to send a lonely beam across the bedspread.

Unable to return to sleep she began to reflect on a recent turn of events. Independence, a strong will and stubborn determination had always been her character traits. After Daniel's death the intense flames of grief had forged these qualities into a protective carapace. She may not pick up a rifle to fight in this war, but she could at least become tougher, morally and emotionally. Surviving, helping support and protect his family was a kind of heroism wasn't it? It was just a different kind of heroism, and she wore the badges of that suffering with fierce pride. When they first met hadn't she just been a typical young girl in love, perhaps simply in love with being in love? There followed the emotional exhaustion of wrangling with his parents who saw only embarrassment and the sheer folly of him wanting to marry a shiksa, and an orphan at that. The experience had eroded her naivety and innocence. But that family turmoil was nothing, was a trivial affair, compared to the German invasion, the abject capitulation of Paris, followed by the exodus south. All those life or death uncertainties made the matter of their unholy marriage seem inconsequential.

Lately she had begun to believe the truth of that phrase trotted out by survivors of the first war - 'the things that do not kill you make you stronger'. And she had become strong. Returning to Paris. Reclaiming the family property. Devising a new routine of living within the surreal landscape of an occupied city. Becoming unexpectedly familiar with the strange day to day customs. Queuing for bread, being ever mindful of what you said to strangers, protecting your bicycle with your life, hurrying to work as a waitress or a clerk when any work could be found. In this way, she thought, she had been strong. She could see a change in her face too. In the mirror, her fair hair - cut shorter now - framed her blue-grey eyes and her face appeared leaner through hunger, her jaw more sharply defined but her lips, though pale, remained soft and full. She did not judge herself too harshly. Until a few weeks ago.

He had always been polite and courteous, she thought. Aloof and stiff at first but then after a while he seemed to mellow a little and began to venture some conversational pleasantries. He fixed the light in the hallway. He shouted at the soldiers in the lower rooms to be quiet. He began to bring her things. Food items mostly. Oranges, eggs, fresh bread, even fresh meat – black market of course, but then he had contacts, he was something to do with the administration of supplies. At first, she took the treasures unquestioningly and cooked them for him. But he began to insist she keep some for herself. She resisted. Until one day he brought the coffee.

Lucienne took some deep breaths and exhaled slowly, trying to let herself drift back off to sleep. But her mind was awake now, restlessly searching for meaning, for justification, for atonement. The scene appeared in her mind, replaying, vivid as a movie.

A simple waxed paper bag containing fresh coffee beans. She hadn't seen or smelled anything like it for four years. From the top of a cabinet she brought down the rusty old grinder, dusted it off and began to pour the beans in, slowly turning the handle. She nearly fainted – the rich smoky aroma entered the room like a long-lost love. Could a simple smell have such a powerful effect? As the deep fragrance filled the room she began to smile, and tears came unbidden into her eyes and began rolling down her cheeks. She fetched Aunt Miriam's ancient coffee pot, carefully spooned in the grains and added the water, wiping the tears from her face with a tea towel. She put the pot on the stove and sat down to recover her emotions. It was so trivial, so bourgeois. Thousands were dying on battlefields and in camps and she was losing her grip over some coffee – it was shameful really. She composed herself and polished a cup ready to pour for him. She had never smiled at him. It was part of her power. But when she called down to him for his coffee and he came up the stairs into her kitchenette he stretched his arms over his head, inhaled deeply, and said, rather theatrically, in his laboured French, *"Le monde est bon, maintenant que nous avons du café frais!"*

His face lit up in a wide, honest, innocent, joyful grin. And despite all her innermost resolve the little muscles on her cheeks refused to lie still and her lips began to curl up at the edges – on some primitive physical level she could not resist the impulse. He insisted she have a cup. She refused.

But this time he went to the shelf, selected a pretty china mug, which she noticed was a chipped leftover from grandma's Meissen, dusted it, went to the stove and poured for her. He passed it graciously to her and said, "*Pour toi Lucienne, une tasse de plaisir.*"

Buying the town-house in the 5th had seemed pretentious to her at the time, an affectation. Yes of course the business was booming in the years before the war but was it really necessary to move outside the Marais? Although she would never be fully accepted, even so, out of respect for her husband's family she had tried her hardest to celebrate the sabbath, to understand halakhah and to observe the Jewish calendar, putting her goy traditions to one side. It seemed that Daniel's parents would never accept her – it was only that he was so successful within the family business that he was allowed to get away with it. And that same success bought the house on Rue Samarande, with its grand doorway, its wine cellars and stone vaults and its elegant tall-ceilinged apartments where two generations could live in harmony without getting in each other's way.

Soon the beauty and grace of the house began to win her over. Aunt Miriam was the fashionable one in Daniel's family. She knew artists and poets, she went to the Opera and to the gallery openings. She took Lucienne on the hunt for antiques and furnishings, speaking knowledgeably of colour palettes and textiles. And she, most of all, accepted Lucienne for who she was and not for her being non-Jewish.

But even as the decorators finished the epic wall-papering and painting and the new heating boiler had been installed in the cellar (you could hear the 'woof' like a small bomb every time it fired up), there began to be heard more and more the talk of Nazism, the threat of war and the persecution and alienation of Jews living in Germany. Hardly had the new rosewood dining table and lyre-back chairs arrived from Le Bon Marché when the news became more serious and the talk of invasion, previously dismissed as scaremongering, became more disturbing and threatening.

Lucienne remembered how it had all happened so quickly. The brave French armies could not withstand the terrible swift might of the German forces. Paris began to fill with refugees. From Belgium and Holland and from the regions of the n

orth they left their homes, arriving in Paris in transit, the stations filled with homeless families boarding special trains to seek safety in the south. They had pitied these refugees at the time. There had been too much talk of surrender and appeasement. 'Surely Paris would stand alone and proudly defy the worst the boches could throw at us?' they had thought. But the rallying cries fell on deaf ears. And what could we do as mere citizens to persuade the politicians and generals not to waiver? Nothing. So, it began. The great exodus.

Dramatic decisions were made in days, even overnight. The cloth factory workers were given the option to leave with a month's pay if they wanted. It was pragmatic – they were nearly all Jews. The shop would stay open as long as possible, staffed by non-Jews, at least until stocks ran out. Then one evening in early June 1940 Grandpa Belman arrived at the house in Rue Samarande and brought one of the factory vans with him. Everyone gathered in the drawing room. Grandpa and grandma. Daniel's parents, his sister, Aunt Miriam, her daughters. It was like a scene from Ibsen or Chekhov – the affluent middle classes surrounded by their finery: venetian mirrors, velvet drapes, crystal chandeliers, modernist paintings by Miriam's Bohemian artist protégés, silk damask canapés and silver-framed portraits on the baby grand piano. But instead of sharing the pleasures and rewards of their hard work in a warm and peaceful moment with family they were discussing the absolutely unthinkable – that they might have to leave the house, to leave Paris. Like one of Miriam's paintings it had a surreal quality, things that had seemed so solid and predictable were now thrown out of alignment and all perspective had been abandoned. They were chattering quietly, urgently amongst each other, exchanging the latest rumours from the street when Daniel's father, Levy, walked over to the curtains and drew them, closing out the remains of the June evening dusk. He stood in front of the mantel-piece and spoke softly and slowly, but with a tone of authority and dignity which Lucienne had not witnessed before.

"My family. Bless you all. We know why we are gathered here. This is a dark time for us, for our family, for Paris. I have consulted with the rabbis and elders. I have listened to stories from the refugees coming through the city. There is a lot of idle talk and wishful thinking about holding back the boches. But there will be no defence. Our city will be handed over to the Germans. We Jews risk everything under the Nazis. We risk our lives, our existence. There is no question. We must all leave the city and go to the cousins in Valence. There is no time to waste. We do not have time to discuss this. I have made the decision. We leave first thing in the morning. I have the van downstairs. We will pack it after dusk. Take only your clothing and your small valuables...anything you treasure or anything you can sell. We don't know how long it will take us or what challenges may befall us. Daniel will drive the Peugeot. Miriam, we will need your car as well. We will all leave together at dawn. The LORD bless you and keep you; the LORD make his face shine upon you and be gracious to you; the LORD turn his face toward you and give you peace."

Lucienne stood in the middle of their beautiful salon on the second floor and wondered how on earth she would choose what to take. What was most precious? Would there be room for artworks, for books? Daniel was already carrying boxes up and down ready to load the cars. Miriam's girls were sitting on the stairs, crying because they had been told to bring only a tiny handful of toys. Everything was an anxious whirl of decision and indecision, of shouts from below and the opening and shutting of armoires and chests and drawers. And in the midst of all this, Daniel's father insisted that anything remotely identifiable as Jewish must be removed from the house! Otherwise they might be traced or identified, or if one day they returned there could be trouble awaiting them. So Daniel loaded the car with everything we could think of. From silk embroidered chests came the Tallits and Tzitzits - prayer shawls and fringes handed down generation to generation - the Hebrew dictionaries and Torahs, Russian ceramics and icons, the Shabbos, the menorah...anything, anything that looked, smelled, tasted remotely Jewish. In the quiet time before dawn he drove to grandpa's old allotment outside the city and buried it all, not wanting to risk being stopped on the road. Later, as dawn broke, with hardly any sleep between them, the whole family gathered in the basement kitchen and said a prayer before walking through the rear garden to the old coach-house where the lorry and two cars were waiting, absurdly loaded with a bizarre melange of treasures and trivia that reflected the panic, yearning, nostalgia and dread that overcame them all.

The shared coffee was nothing, a friendly gesture, yet it contained everything that came later. It was a catharsis, a release of tension, but it was also a transgression, a deviation. He offered the china cup to her, the steamy aromatic vapours rising like a genie from a lamp, and she took it from him with both hands, and she smiled, ever so slightly, but it could not be denied.

She had been defiant in a quiet, determined way. When she returned to Paris in '43 there were the stirrings of doubt in the German ranks about the progress of the war. With forged identity papers and carefully adapted title deeds showing her name as Lucienne Bell she proved ownership of the house and was able to dislodge the German soldiers billeted in the upper apartment, though the lower floors remained occupied. Surprisingly, the fabric of the house was still in reasonable condition, although most of the valuable furniture, the piano, the crystal chandeliers and some of the artworks had gone.

From the bucolic distant valleys of the Southern Rhône

it had been easy to hate the Germans. It hadn't taken long for news to reach them of the callous disregard for prisoners, about the brutal treatment of the Jewish communities and the camps. They had heard about the round-up and deportation of Jews at the Vélodrome d'Hiver. There were rumours of buses leaving Nice packed with Jewish citizens, some of them betrayed by once good neighbours. But here, back in Paris, there existed an un-worldly, unethical spirit of compromise between the occupiers and the occupied, an air of shared destiny, even a mutual understanding, which Lucienne found shocking. How could you go to work in a German armaments factory? How could some women dress up and be escorted to the movies or the theatre on the arms of Nazi officers? How could you even ride your bike along the street as German soldiers went about their everyday business right next to you?

But she realised soon enough that there was no choice for most citizens. Unless you were brave enough to join a Resistance cell and risk your life then you had little option. From the relative bounty of a country farm she found the food rationing and the extortionate black market of Paris difficult to tolerate. But people were thin and hungry, so they queued for bread and they ventured out into the fields of the suburbs to scrounge farm foods and firewood. And those with weaker wills succumbed to the temptations of becoming collaborators and informers.

Lucienne's act of resistance was her return to the family house, to a property secretly owned by Jews. She resolved never to abandon the house again. Her defiance was manifest in the hatred within her eyes and in the haughty way she looked at the scruffy soldiers occupying the lower apartment. She was bold enough to give them orders, to stop leaving rubbish on the steps, to clean their mess on the floors, to stop shouting at night and not bring women into the house. They scoffed and laughed at her, but she could see they were intimidated, some of them no more than boys.

Paris had become a nightmarish version of itself. Street signs in gothic German lettering. Giant swastika flags on public buildings. Horses and carriages returned to the streets. There was less traffic noise - you could hear birdsong even as you cycled to work or queued with your rationbook. By nine in the evening it was even quieter due to the curfew. The eerie spell would only be broken by the wail of air-raid sirens.

Then one day Oberstleutnant Neumann arrived and took over the second floor for his digs, moving into her precious salon. She had no say in the matter of course, not even time to move out any of the remaining furniture or paintings. From the start she remained detached and reserved – he was simply another necessary evil which could be thwarted in her own way. But he surprised her and defied her expectations. Injured on the Russian front, he had been transferred to a desk job at the administrative headquarters which now occupied a former hotel on the Champs-Elysées. When he was out during the day she sometimes ventured into his room, her old salon, using her spare key to unlock the door and moving cautiously so as not to disturb anything. The Brittany seascape remained perched on the mantelpiece, the velvet cushions were still scattered on grandma's old sofa. But there was now a single metal bed, a utilitarian desk with a typewriter and a table with two chairs in the corner. He had added some personal items; simple framed photos of a woman and two children, a scarlet geranium in a terracotta pot, some prints and postcards - a scene of Provence, a Vermeer, a Klimt. She noted too a growing collection of books; Hardy, Keats, Tolstoy, Baudelaire, Freud, Jung – some in German, some in English or French. He had taken the bathroom on the landing for his private ablutions and she noticed with irritation how neat and tidy he kept it. The razor and brush placed just so on the mirrored shelf, fine Marseille soap always to hand and a sleek bottle of Dunhill eau-de-cologne.

She was obliged to make him breakfast and dinner which he took at the table in his room. He began to return in the evenings with black market foods and treats which she cooked but refused to share. She observed him surreptitiously during these moments in his room. He would remove his stiff officer's jacket – that June was unusually hot – and roll up his shirt sleeves. He would open the window and lean out to have a smoke. There was a melancholic air about him, she decided. He was infinitely patient and polite with her, never demanding, but he looked like a man whose life has been left behind, perhaps on a battlefield or perhaps at the Tyrolean house that she saw in the background of his family photos.

At first it was all 'Frau Bell' and 'Oberstleutnant Neumann' between them, but after a month of formalities, one day as she brought him his dinner he said, "Look, let us be civilised people, of course there is a war but still you are also a hostess and I a guest and we should get along in a civilised manner, don't you think?" With this he stood up and gave a sort of ironic bow and re-introduced himself. "Abelard," he said. "And may I call you Lucienne?"

She was flummoxed by this unexpected gesture and said simply, "If you wish." But she continued to refer to him as Herr Neumann.

They began to have short conversations, about the weather, about Paris. He asked questions about her family, her past, what she did before the war, was she married? Lucienne did her best to give brief answers without appearing evasive. One evening, he said, "It is such a fine evening and so hot indoors – shall we take a stroll along the streets, or to the park?"

"You know that it is not possible for me."

And Abelard replied, "Everything is possible. Especially if I say so."

As he said this he smiled at her, but this time his smile seemed mischievous, perhaps even malign, and he didn't seem himself. He looked around the room and said, "This is indeed a beautiful house. You are fortunate to own a house like this. Do you know that in my work we have files and files, tens of thousands of files, records of houses in Paris bought and houses sold, records of people coming and going, births and deaths. You would be surprised what information is under lock and key in my headquarters. Perhaps I should have a look and find out more about the history of a house like this. Who was the architect and the builder who created such finery, who lived here in centuries gone by, who lived here before the war. It would be fascinating don't you think? Everything is possible."

Not long after that, her nightmares began. Running along alien city streets where giant Swastika flags flew from buildings or from the balcony of her house, air raid sirens wailing, her swearing in guttural German at the people below. Or digging in the allotment, using her bare hands in the mud, looking for the family treasures, finding only rotten human bones and iron crosses.

When everyone was out of the house she searched it compulsively, top to bottom, attic to cellar, looking for clues or anything that would give away Daniel's family. Was there something Jewish about the curtains and the fabrics? Was there something about the ovens or the utensils? Had anything been left behind in wardrobes? Did the house smell of scented candles or baking challah bread? Were there any clues in the garden shed to the existence of the allotment? She almost wanted to scour the floors and walls with bleach to remove any possible stain or trace. She replayed what he had said over and over in her mind. Yet as the weeks passed he never spoke the same way again and she began to wonder if his meaning was entirely innocent... it was so out of keeping. Then came the coffee, and worse, she started to call him Abelard.

Lucienne recalled the exodus from Paris - an ordeal of almost biblical proportions. When their little convoy left the coach-house she took one last look from the car back at the tall windows of the house, starting to reflect the early dawn light. Then they were gone. The family had together managed to conjure up a sort of *esprit de guerre*, as if they were all going on a great holiday venture. Ostensibly this was for the benefit of her young nieces, but it served to give everyone an initial sense of purpose and resilience. It didn't last long. They had hardly reached the suburbs when it became abundantly clear that half the population of Paris was headed south, by all and any means possible. A ragtag caravanserai of hand-drawn carts, ponies, donkeys, bicycles and every kind of motorised transport, lorries, buses, delivery wagons, cars of all sizes laden with cases and trunks and paraphernalia, some with mattresses strapped to their roofs; farm vehicles, motorbikes, tractors, wheelbarrows - anything with wheels - all jostled with each other to stay on the choked roads. People were even pushing prams laden with possessions and sometimes with children or old folk clinging on desperately. Men carried suitcases and great cloth sacks slung over their shoulders. To save carrying more clothes many people wore their suits and coats but were soon suffering in the heatwave. And always the same grim, resigned expressions. And always the same questions. Are there any trains? Is anyone here a doctor? Does anyone know if they have gasoline in the next town?

Progress was painstakingly slow. Many were heading for Rouen, so Daniel's grandpa suggested taking a different road and eventually they passed the slower refugees and started to make a little better progress. Later they met French army trucks heading north and one time just outside a little village they came under serious air attack. The planes raced in from the East dropping bombs on the road and strafing the convoy of cars and army vehicles. Everyone jumped out of the cars and dived into the ditch to take cover. Lucienne witnessed many people killed or maimed that day, but the family were fortunate only to have scratches from the brambles and debris.

Ten days later, they arrived at the family farm near Valence. They had just the factory lorry left, with barely enough gasoline for another few kilometres. They were dirty, physically drained and demoralised. Possessions had been abandoned or bartered along the way. One of the children seemed shell-shocked or traumatised but otherwise they were all over-joyed to reach safety and the warmth of Provençal sunshine and family embraces.

Everyone adapted to life in the country except Daniel, and Lucienne began to see a profound change in her husband. He complained endlessly about the war, about the Vichy government, about the corrupt officials, and most of all about the German occupation of his beloved country and their treatment of the Jewish populations. It bred in him a deep bitterness, a resentment which made his everyday manner aggressive and sharp. It was as if he seemed to be substituting his former business energies with a kind of crazed determination to fight back in some small way. He began to disappear on secretive journeys for a few days. It was dressed up as business affairs but everyone in the family suspected he was becoming involved in the resistance effort.

That winter Lucienne began to question whether she could truly love a man whose fire was now kindled not by his wife but by a passion to disrupt or destroy an enemy that represented the epitome of evil in his eyes. Later, older and wiser, she would regret ever having doubted Daniel in this way, because in the spring of 41, he failed to return home after some sort of secret resistance mission in Marseille. A week after his disappearance a stranger arrived at the farm, walked slowly to the farmhouse with his hat in his hand, came quietly into the front room and gave them the solemn news. Daniel had died a hero, helping important people escape from the port, but despite their best efforts, they were over-run and could not return to recover his body.

Lucienne spent six seasons more in the south, alternating between her foster family's house in the Ardèche and Daniel's family farm near Valence. At first the gentle rhythm of the country seasons was a balm to her grief. She could lose herself in the everyday tactile routines of the farm and the sights and sounds of the countryside. But as her grief waned so the consciousness of the war re-entered her mind and she began to think back to her life before the war, to Paris, to the dreams she and Daniel had shared, to the house on Rue Samarande. She was childless, a widow. What was she doing living this barren life in the country. Where was her spirit, her resistance?

When Abelard changed his uniform for off-duty clothes he seemed to Lucienne to be at heart a kind, thoughtful family man. He told her about the fighting in Russia, how he had been injured by shrapnel in the shoulder and back. He never said that he regretted being called up, or discussed politics, but she sensed that he was a victim of his time, that he had no choice in the matter. Although she refused his invitations to walk in the park they began to eat together some evenings at the table in his room, especially when he returned with one of his packages containing a treat - a fresh fish, a cake, a bottle of Bordeaux. By some unspoken pact, their conversations remained on neutral ground – places they had visited, summers before the war.

"One day you should visit the south, Abelard. Don't go to the Riviera, go to the hills of Provence or the Ardèche," Lucienne reminisced, as Abelard sat back in his chair, swirling the wine in his glass. "In the early summer is best. In the garrigue you walk on old stone paths that shepherds have walked for centuries, across plateaux of ochre stone where the wild goats live, or down through terraces of ancient olives. And the scents! As you walk your boots will brush the wild thyme and rosemary – I can smell them now. And if you know where to look there is juniper and sometimes fennel. We collected them all and my auntie would add them to the pot to make a mouth-watering stew or if we found myrtle she would crush the leaves to make oil and keep it in her medicine cupboard."

Abelard was entranced and insisted she go on. Taking another sip of red wine, she continued, "I remember, one time, the summer was so hot, and we were running through the dry grass behind our farm. I was with my cousins and as we ran wave after wave of cicadas would leap ahead of us like sprays of fireworks. And the heat! It was drummed into us to always take a water bottle; we roamed so freely, hardly seeing another soul except an old shepherd or two. The best thing was when the sun had warmed your head and shoulders like they were fried in a pan then we would go down into the valleys to look among the rocks and find a spring, bursting with cool mountain water, and quench our thirst, or even take off our clothes and swim in the rock pools."

Lucienne felt a tinge of embarrassment at this talk of swimming naked, so she turned the conversation around and asked Abelard what he remembered best from before the war.

After a pause, Abelard spoke quietly, "In truth, my favourite memory is from a holiday I took with my family in the Schwarzwald. I don't wish to imply that home-life on our farm was bad in anyway. On the contrary I miss it every day, but there were special moments on this holiday – perhaps we all need to be away from the routine of everyday life to appreciate each other. We stayed in a big guest-house, like a chalet-hotel high in the hills. From our balcony you could smell the pine forest and almost touch the trees. You probably know that we Germans feel a special kinship with the forest? As children so many of our fables and bedtime stories are laced with woodsmen and hunters and castles and beautiful women."

As he said this, Abelard raised his glass to Lucienne, and continued, "The children met new friends and played all day, and Elfrida and I were free. To walk in the hills or swim in the lake. To take a picnic and lie in the sun. To make love in the afternoon and no children to disturb us!"

One such evening during the winter, with early snow falling on the city streets, they dined together and drank several glasses of a fine wine he had acquired from a restaurateur. After saying good-night and preparing to go to bed in her attic bedroom, Lucienne realised that she had left her reading glasses on the table in Abelard's room. She tiptoed barefoot downstairs, knocked quietly on his door and entered the room a little too quickly, where she found Abelard with his shirt removed, massaging oil into his shoulder. The wound was shocking, a wide purple scar running from his shoulder down to the back of his ribcage, the skin pulled and bunched in awkward knots where they had carried out crude repairs in the field hospital.

It had been a pleasant evening and the wine had made her mellow and relaxed. Instead of apologising and walking out, she approached him and took the bottle of oil from his hand. No words were spoken. She poured a spoonful of oil into the hollow of her palm and poured it gently onto his broad shoulders. The wound was a dreadful thing to behold, ugly and cruel, though to her touch it was warm and yielding. There was no sound in the room other than their breathing and the slight rustle of her dress as she moved forward and back with each sweep of her hand. Abelard reached his hand up and grasped hers. Then he stood up and turned to face her, his cheeks wet with tears.

Later, looking back, she wondered if that was really the moment when it began, or was it the coffee, or was it when she feared he knew about her family? Would she ever really know or understand from what impulse, from what need, the ripples of desire emanated?

But desire it was, the passion more inflamed now by her earlier painstaking efforts to avoid thinking of him as a man, as human even. Their lovemaking was urgent and abandoned, all moralities thrown aside like the cast-off clothing at the foot of the bed. Lying on her back she ran her fingers across his shoulders, across the scar, even as he lunged into her again and again, so that she wanted it all, all his lust and all his pain. And Abelard felt himself lost on a journey, a journey to an exquisite star, now with his eyes closed imagining he was with his wife, or now with a red-lipped whore in the brothel, or now with all women through all time, and then with his eyes open, looking into Lucienne's eyes, for once soft and tender, where he could see her desire and her need to be possessed.

Together they entered a kind of mutual madness. The war was madness. Their situation was madness. They became like children on a roller-coaster or a ghost-train; they had departed and there was no turning back. Together they rode the swoops and turns of their secret affair, and together they frightened and thrilled each other with dangerous talk of alternative futures and secret escapes. But they both knew it was all a folly, a game of insanity in a world turned upside down.

But Lucienne's madness was not the same as Abelard's. For Abelard returned each day to the rational order and moral superiority of his office colleagues, and he quietly believed that one day he would return to his wife, that he would have his army pension and he would tend the farm and watch the children growing up. And Lucienne, where would she be?

Lucienne's mind was twisted, all her thoughts were

knotted to the point where she hardly knew what she believed or felt. What did she feel? Was she a cherished possession or a frivolous plaything? A plaything or a cheap whore, excited by the black-market trinkets and delicacies that paid for her services? Yet she loved him for it, for his care and his attention, so absent from her soul since Daniel had gone. For the tenderness of his touch, for the goodness in his heart, for his longing for his family. Yet she hated him too. For being a German officer, for invading her city, for the cruelty of his people, for occupying her house, for possessing her. Surely this was a betrayal of everything she held precious? Of pride and honour, of her love for her husband? But she was a woman, alone, lonely, in a mad tragedy of a life and Abelard, a man, just a man, damaged, at the mercy of fate.

She pictured his future, returning victorious to his village in Bavaria, to the open arms of his wife and children, the hero adorned with garlands and medals. And what of her future? Would she be the sad grey-haired woman running a chambre d'hôte for German couples holidaying in Paris, their Paris? The one with a guilty secret, her joie de vivre annihilated, her soul scorched, moments of happiness rationed like food?

All through that winter and into the early spring of 1944 they were together like lovebirds in a cage, trying to ignore the outside world until it could be ignored no more. On her errands to find food, on her walks to the café where she worked, Lucienne noticed a change in the atmosphere on the street. Parisians gathered together on street corners and openly exchanged news of the latest battles, the Germans defeated in Africa, in Italy. On the boulevards there was a new sense of urgency. Soldiers were being mobilised and could be seen leaving the city on transport trucks. There more ambulances and hospital vehicles.

Abelard refused to tell her what was happening. If she questioned him he would clam up or tell her to use her eyes and ears. Once he warned her that if the Allies attacked Paris she should leave immediately and go back to her family because the Führer had ordered the complete destruction of the city. As spring turned to summer there was growing talk on the streets of *not if but when* the Allies would break through. Two women she knew had joined the resistance – small acts of sabotage were carried out, anything to interrupt German plans. They were so brave these young women – what had she done to help them? Was she at best a collaborator, for giving her time and affection to the enemy?

Abelard had become tense as the news came in of Allied successes. He worked late and chose not to come to her bed so often. He brought less gifts and treats – he said it had become more difficult to obtain food. He would sit at his desk late at night drinking brandy. He didn't want to talk except to warn her. "You haven't told anyone about us, have you? There will be reprisals. If we must leave, our soldiers will be angry; stay indoors as much as you can. They are looking to round up more Jews wherever they can find them – if you have Jewish friends, if any are still in hiding, God help them."

One day in July Abelard went to work and never returned. During the day a lorry arrived, and two soldiers collected all his papers and personal items. She stood on the stairs, shouting at them, asking them what was going on, where was Herr Neumann? But they pushed past her and left without saying a word. For several days she imagined Abelard would come in to say goodbye, just a few words, but there was nothing. With the soldiers on the ground floor already gone, suddenly the big house was silent and empty.

August 1944 was the final turning point. Partisans and resistance groups were mobilising. Posters appeared calling Parisians to rise up against the retreating Germans. Barricades appeared, people were on the streets, tricolours waved at windows, even as snipers fired at civilians. By the end of August, it was over, the French and Americans were greeted with ecstatic crowds, the Germans formally surrendered, and De Gaulle returned to Paris.

Lucienne joined in the celebrations with her friends, but

her joy was still tarnished by thoughts of Abelard. Would he have escaped back to his family? Would he have been forced to fight a desperate rear-guard battle on the final fronts of the war – they said Hitler had called up boys of fifteen and old men of seventy, anyone who could carry a weapon. And once, with horror, she saw an angry mob marching a woman to a public square where a baying crowd shouted vile names at the woman and a man shaved off her hair and held up her face, so they could all witness and identify the collaborator.

She told herself that her affair with Abelard had been a private and innocent collaboration, a mingling of two souls with no allegiance to country or cause. But still it made her uneasy and she spent her time in the weeks following the liberation working in the garden, tidying and cleaning the house, trying to enjoy the simple pleasures of being in her unoccupied home. She wrote letters to her foster family and to Daniel's family, wondering if it was now safe to visit and whether, God willing, one day soon they might return to Paris. She yearned to see them all, to walk in the garrigue again, but until then she would remain the guardian and protector of the house.

One morning she woke early, thinking of Abelard. The news for the Germans was grim, they were still fighting to the bitter end. She had not used his room, her old salon, since he had left, just cleaning it and dusting it, preferring to stay in her nest on the top floor. But that morning she went downstairs and looked again at the bare boards, the marks on the rug where his desk and chair had stood, at the small table in the corner where they had shared meals. She looked at the painting that stood on the mantelpiece, protected by dusty glass. It was nothing exciting, a seascape of Brittany, a pleasant watercolour. It was strange that it had never been hung properly. Daniel or Grandpa must have put it there in their haste when we abandoned the house, she thought. She took it down to look at the back to see if it had an inscription. Behind where the painting had rested she was surprised to see a postcard sitting on the mantelpiece. On the front was a scene of the Moulin Rouge, an old black and white photo with hand colouring, but it was the writing on the back which almost stopped her heart.

*'I never told anyone. You will be safe now I think. God help us. Have a good life mon amour'.*

It was signed 'A'.

She sat down on the old sofa and held the card to her chest, so many thoughts racing through her mind, her heart beating wildly. She looked over to where the painting had stood on the mantel. There were strange soft brown marks on the wall, seven little finger-print sized shadows in a neat line from left to right, with one slightly higher in the centre. She rose to examine them. And as she went up closer it dawned on her with a kind of dreadful anticipation, that she knew what this pattern was, and she feared with a chill dark fear what it meant. The marks were the faintest burns, the soft, sooty heat trails emitted by seven candles. This was where Daniel and she had placed the silver menorah candle-holder when they moved into the apartment. This was where she had taken pleasure in lighting the candles to show him her respect for his religion. Her mind returned to the time of their exodus and she pictured Daniel seeing these marks on his way out of the building during their hasty departure, grabbing the painting and putting it on the mantelpiece. And on her return to Paris she had scoured the house for every possible sign, every trace of their religion, but had never thought to look behind this simple painting.

She touched the candle marks on the wall and closed her eyes, as if in prayer. She imagined she was touching Daniel's fingertips. She was touching the cool dark earth of the allotment where the menorah was buried, touching all the good people that once lived in this house together in the warmth of God and family, reaching out in supplication to her foster parents and to the new family that Daniel had given her, and to all the other Jewish fathers and mothers, grandparents, uncles and aunts, brothers and sisters, sons and daughters betrayed and lost in the maelstrom of war.

"Bless you all", she whispered, "and forgive my sin".

# Les Années Folles

## Argenteuil, near Paris, October 1963

Outside her window the afternoon sun shines through an old plane tree, turning the leaves incandescent yellow. Today, almost for the first time in years, Elodie feels in her chest a swell of emotion that could only be described as a kind of happiness. She thinks, 'He is coming! Finally, I can't believe it, Serge is really coming! My boy, my darling boy is coming this very day! Look at this old iron bed-frame where I lie, on a lumpy worn out mattress, in this eerie place, visited only by nuns and doctors. Who would imagine happiness can be found here?'

On this late October day, she feels her weary spirit rising luminously within her and, although she is not devout, she fingers the rosary beads the nuns have given her and says to herself again and again 'he is coming', like a mantra. She whispers to one of the nurses, "Come closer Sister Dorothée, I will tell you a scandalous secret for nothing. You see, he was my lovechild and his father so handsome! Wait until you see him, you will swoon, I promise!"

She has shared this precious secret with all the Sisters, but their hallowed minds rise above such earthly fables. They respond with their wan, unworldly smiles because, she supposes, they believe that God gives, and God takes away and nothing she or Serge can do will change a thing. But still she teases them anyway, even though they pretend not to hear, gliding along corridors, quietly communing with each other, pressing down their starched linen smocks.

Elodie's thoughts form and change shape like summer clouds sweeping over the dome of Sacré-Coeur. 'Where has he been? America for sure, I know that much, but since then? Hardly a call or a letter for the first few years and then nothing, nothing for eight years! Ah but why would he? He blames me I know. I chose badly – I know it but what could I have done? I was a young girl with a little boy – hardly catch of the day. So, I chose badly. So, I was desperate. And you paid the price much more than me. But you have no idea what really happened. How much I must tell you, now before it is too late. Will I have the courage to tell you? I must, I must. Because you are coming, coming to see your Mama. I see your face, the sweet, smooth face of the innocent boy I adored and the suave, tanned face of the young man in navy uniform. The faces blend, now I see a phantom picture of you, it is so hard to imagine the reality. Perhaps your face will be lined with age - but will it be free of cares or frowned with sadness?'

She clutches his postcard; it is the Baie des Anges in Nice. Sunshine, palm trees and the cerulean blue of the sea. The stamp is a coat of arms with fleurs de lys. The card is now creased and stained from being held so close to her heart. She can't resist reading it again although she could recite the words from memory, like a psalm.

*Dear Elodie,*

*I have been away, but I received your last letter. I am sorry to hear you are unwell. I will arrive by train on Thursday 28 October and come to see you in the afternoon.*
*With affection*
*Serge*

She thinks 'Elodie, Elodie, why does he call me Elodie? What happened to Maman? I suppose he must still blame me - it's obvious. But still he is coming. Serge is really coming today, this afternoon, he is arriving by train . . . he sends me his affection. It is not nothing, this affection. To have affection from your son. It won't cure me but still if this affection could become love, if only for a moment, like an ember coaxed into a gentle flame, then what might happen? My body is done for, but what of my soul? Could it be sanctified by such a brief glow of redemptive love?'

She drifts into another sleep, induced by the morphine. But these are not normal sleeps. They are the restless sleeps of lost souls endlessly tumbling off the edge of the world, reaching out over and over with long yearning fingers grasping at the trailing shrouds of life. When she wakes, one hand is clasping the faded embroidery of the white sheet and the other still holds the postcard. The sun is streaming through the window as Sister Dorothée wipes her brow with cool wet cotton.

Serge notices how his fellow passengers on the train seem to do a lot of day-dreaming. When you catch their eye, their looks are glazed and distant or they stare endlessly out of the windows at passing villages and fields. He tries to avoid this type of behaviour, finding it neither productive nor stimulating. He is used to travelling with companions, a girlfriend to entertain him or a business associate with whom to make plans. Today, this unexpected mission has caught him off-guard. He has read the newspaper cover to cover and made notes about his business project with neat writing in a small leather pocket-book. With an hour to go before Paris he tries to occupy his mind; he examines the tiny details of the fabrication of the metal fittings, the chrome window winder, the ashtray with its sooty indentations, the brass coat-rack and the faded travel labels on the leather luggage stored above the seats. But his search for distraction is short-lived.

Things were moving along nicely with his new venture and then these letters from his mother arrived, forwarded from America. She is unwell. Can he visit her? He feels like he has been derailed. His thoughts are harder to control than normal and with nothing else to occupy it, his mind begins to wander like a stubborn old dog rooting around in the thickets and curious undergrowth of his memory.

He is thirty-seven years old now. He knows himself well enough. After the war he went a bit wild. The freedom, the chance to be his own person, to come out of the long shadows cast by his father – he exorcised his past with a savage exuberance. The car business in Paris, the clubs, the girls, the thrill of survivors being re-born into a brave post-war world. But he was a dilettante and he paid the price. He lost money, he drank too much, sacrificed his marriage - he was out of control.

Now after the years of graft in America he is back in France and managing to hold it all together. Now he is like the estate keeper, busy checking the boundaries of his life, keeping the wildness at bay and always putting on a good display for visitors. He has the discipline he gained during the war. He has the logic and strategy of a smart businessman. It's a routine and he has it to a tee. But he is wise enough to know too that the secret hurtful places are always there, out of bounds. Some of his memories still stalk him, waiting for an opportunity to strike. He doesn't kid himself. You can lock them up and hide them from view, you can throw away the key, but they never completely disappear, these demons. It's always the same pattern of thought that plagues him. 'Why did she fall for him in the first place, the controlling little shit that he was. Was it just because she was poor, and Henri had the income, the government job, respectability, the holiday house in Fréjus? Was it the money or did he get her pregnant? Pregnant with yours truly. Of course, that would have been it – the marriage to avoid the shame, but what made her love him? Could she not see how I came to despise him because he didn't spend time with me like other kids fathers, didn't seem to love me the way a father should, so that in the end I hated to call him Papa, and it stuck to my teeth saying that word, and he knew I detested him and I started to call him Henri, but he made me say Papa all the time just to grind me down, to let me know he was the boss, he was the man in her life, not me. And when the verbal abuse didn't gain him enough respect well he knew what to do. Did she know? She must have known, yet she stuck with him. How could she?'

In the fields outside the train, Serge notices a ray of gold emerge from a cloud to illuminate a meadow of late hay, but his mind wanders again. Fréjus. I must have been seven or eight. God, those summers when Henri stayed to work in Paris and me and Mama had the peace of the little whitewashed cottage, the whole beautiful beach, the clouds, the sun and rain, the wide sky was ours alone. The day I was brave enough to swim in the cove and dive down to pick up my first *oursin*, a glossy spiny sea-urchin, and wrapped it in my towel and ran back through the hot sandy lanes my heart thumping with pride. And Mama was in the garden, hanging striped sheets on the line and I saw her with the sun in her hair between the billowing sheets and I loved her more in that moment because I knew we were special, we were together without him and I was about to show her my prize and I knew she would kneel and laugh and smile and hug me and nothing could ever be so perfect. In fact, after that summer it was never perfect again, it was terrible. How could she live with him, how could she not see my pain and how my love for her died every time she kissed him, every time she cooked him his favourite dinner, every time she took his arm in the park and I wanted to run away. And one day I did.

The train lurches as they enter the goods yards and sidings near the Gare Saint-Lazare. He feels irritated for allowing his mind to drift back to the bad times and tells himself to get a grip.

He takes the suburban train to Argenteuil and walks

from the station to the address she gave. He is surprised to find himself standing in front of a large crumbling, institutional building with the words "Hotel-Dieu Argenteuil" carved long ago onto a stone arch, but with numerous more modern hospital signs attached. She had said she was poorly, but the signs suggested something more ominous and the building itself looked gloomy and imposing. As he crosses the threshold he wishes for his self-control to be at its sharpest, but he finds instead that his nerves are unsettled, and unfamiliar emotions are slinking like eels below the surface of a muddy pond.

On the ward one of the sisters greets him. He asks after his mother and the nurse simply stares into his eyes with a profound gaze which he finds hard to interpret, and she says, "She has been waiting a long time to see you." But then she takes him aside and explains that Elodie has cancer, that it started in her womb, but it was caught too late and has now spread through her body.

He enters her room and could not be more shocked. She seems so small. Like a frail wounded bird. Her skin is yellowish, her hair grey and white, but still long. She hasn't seen him yet, her eyes still shut. He stands for another moment, trying to take it all in, the hospital bed, the faded armchair, the drip which leads to the vein in her arm, the slanting shafts of amber light crossing the room from where a blind has been drawn down at the window. His mother. He barely recognises her.

Elodie is semi-conscious, yet aware of her own thoughts. 'Am I awake or dreaming, or day-dreaming? There's a stony beach and I'm reaching up to some cliffs. I must climb up. I hear the tide coming in behind me, the waves racing up the shingle. A voice. A voice in my dream? A voice in the room, near me?'

Then the voice spoke softly, "Elodie?"

She heard the voice again and then she felt a warm hand on her arm.

The voice spoke again, only this time it said "Maman?"

She hardly dared to open her eyes in case it was only a dream and there would be nothing and no-one in the room. Perhaps she could stay in the dream and it would be the best of dreams, a dream to inhabit forever. The drugs played devilish tricks. But the temptation to find out was too great. Could it be Serge? She opened her eyes and gasped at the revelation of what she was seeing in front of her. She was looking straight into the dark eyes and handsome face of her son, her boy - her missing boy had returned.

For some minutes there were no words between them, for what words could be found to express their feelings? There were tears in Elodie's eyes, running down her cheeks and Serge took out a handkerchief and dabbed at her face and then he too found himself struggling to hold himself together.

Eventually, Elodie began to speak.

"I can't believe it! Mon dieu, I can't believe it's you! You look so well, so well and so handsome, you were always a good-looking boy, my Serge! So much to say to you, but alas not so much time, silly me with this damned illness. I didn't want you to see me like this. But I had to talk to you, there are things, things to tell, so hard to know where to start . . ."

"Don't trouble yourself Maman, I'm here now and we have time," replied Serge, even as he began to wonder how long she really did have. And before he could think of anything more to say – what *do* you say – Elodie carried on.

"I am so sorry we have not seen each other. No, no, don't think it is your fault, it is all mine really and I wanted to see you many, many times, but then the war and then you went to America and, well, we get on with our lives, don't we? Where does it go, the time? I once thought I had forever!"

Elodie took a sip of water and kept looking into Serge's eyes even as she tipped the cup back with shaking hands, so pleased was she to see him again. What was it she saw in his eyes? The little boy, the angry man? Something broken?

"Did they tell you? About what I have? My illness? You do know?" she asked.

Serge nodded and said, "Yes, yes they did. I guessed it

must be serious, but not cancer. I didn't expect that. I am so sorry for you. It's so, so unfair."

"But now you are here, my boy, and that's all that matters. Maybe it is unfair, but life is not fair is it? I learned this a long time ago! Tell me, are you still married? Have you moved back to France permanently?"

"Yes, I have been working in America on and off, but now I have a place in the south and I have brought my business back to France, you would be proud of me! As for marriage, yes, I did marry, but it didn't work out, an American girl, so she took me to the States to live but, well, we were too different, we couldn't get along. It's a long story, complicated. But listen, maybe I'll marry a French girl next time! Or maybe I prefer my own company, who knows? There was someone years ago I still think about, it was after the war – do you remember Jeanne? I should never have let that one go. Anyway, I am fine, really, I am fine. Don't worry about me."

And they talked for a while until she became tired and started to slip back lower and lower in the bed and then she said, "Let me rest for a few hours. Go and take some air, then promise me you will come back. I need to tell you things, important things."

Serge went across the road from the hospital and bought cigarettes. He hadn't smoked in many years but now he sat on a bench and smoked three in a row as he tried to make sense of it all. The unfamiliar sensations of smoking made his eyes water, but he persisted until he could feel the nicotine in his blood-stream; he needed it, anything to take the edge off, to settle his mind, but the thoughts kept coming. 'How long had she got? What has she been doing all these last years? Shall I tell her how I felt about Henri?' In truth Serge was relieved and glad that the bastard had been killed in the war. But still, the anger lingered in his thoughts, 'She could have stopped it, couldn't she? She could have left Henri and the two of us could have escaped. For Christ's sake why didn't she see how bad it was for me?'

Gradually, calming down, he began to question his motives - how could he be so selfish to blame her now when she is fading away from this world? She can't help him now. What could she possibly say? And he can't help her either at this late stage . . . what could *he* say? God, what a mess.

In the hospital, Elodie fell back into a reverie, a kind of euphoria washing over her. Her mind seemed able to drift as freely as pollen carried by summer bees, alighting on impressions and memories, lightly touching and then moving on.

She drifted into memories of Serge as a child, the feel of his little hand in hers as he skipped along the lanes, the simple pleasure they found in each other's company. And as one thought evaporated another came softly to take its place. A strange sensation, of being in control yet not knowing what might happen and whose face would appear in her waking dreams. Back, back she went to a time before Serge and Henri (whose face, in all honesty, she hoped not to see), to Paris in the 20's, the Années Folles they called it, to a time she remembered now in her fading mind as if opening a musical box and being transported gently back accompanied by the poignant melodies of Chopin or Debussy.

Back, back, she winds her way, back to the characters who seemed so much more fascinating than the people she met later in life.

The émigrés from Russia – the White Russians! They had all fled after the Revolution, they had all been supporters of the Tsar. And Ludmilla, dearest Ludmilla, with her oval face and auburn hair, and all her glamorous parties.

Back, back and Elodie knows well where she wants this strange journey to go and whose face must appear, the one face she wants never to die for, but to live, live again if only she could, to hold that face in her hands again and laugh and love again like there is no tomorrow.

'How will he appear to me this time,' she dreams, 'will he come to me alone, the way it was when the party ended, with his flashing deep brown eyes, with his long dark wavy hair. Will he enthral me once more with his energy and charm. Can I be captivated again, even now? I see Ludmilla and her pretty friends, everyone laughing, and here is Stanny, young and handsome and mad with life. I see him the way I saw him the very first time, but now he is going away, down a long corridor, and he is with a young boy this time, like a faded photograph I see only their shapes walking into bright light. Such bright light, such peace.'

Serge returned that afternoon, but the nurses said he had best come again the next day. His mother was in a deep sleep, exhausted. They took his number at the hotel and promised to call if there was any serious change in her condition. In his room at the hotel, he lay on the bed, smoking a cigarette and looking up at the ceiling. What could she possibly tell him that would change anything? And could he even begin to tell her of his reasons for leaving? What would it serve? Of course, if there was any justice then she deserved to hear, to hear how hard it had been for him, to answer the fundamental questions - why? Why did she marry the bastard and why did she stay with him?

But seeing her there, so frail, so thin, her skin bruised like fallen fruit, her pitiful need to see him, really, what would it serve? To make him feel better? To punish her? Life was cruel. It had been tough for him, but he had survived. Unlike her, he had his years ahead, his plans and ambitions still, and what did she have now?

## LES ANNÉES FOLLES

That night, he dreamed he was in Paris again, on a wide boulevard, driving the big Mercedes convertible he had picked up cheap after the war. Jeanne was sitting next to him, wearing a scarf to keep her hair from blowing and in the back were two strangers giving him directions.

The following morning, he returned to the hospital and was surprised and pleased to find Elodie sitting up, perched against a pillow.

"What joy to see you again" she said, "I cannot tell you how much it means. To see your face as handsome as ever, to hold your hand. It is too much."

There was a glimmer of renewed determination and purpose in her eyes. Perhaps they had given her a shot of something? She paused for a moment and gestured towards the glass of water. After taking a few sips, she said, "I have something to tell you, something I have kept as a secret from you which I must tell you now before it is too late."

Serge sat next to her, perched on the edge of the small armchair, holding her hand, as she continued.

"Before the war, I mean back in the twenties, my life was very different to what you remember as a boy. Paris was a thrilling place to be - France had suffered so much in the Great War. You know that your grandfather was killed, and my mother never truly recovered.

"Well, one night there was a party in a wonderful big

apartment, it was on the Rue de Vaugirard. Pretty girls, everyone drinking champagne and vodka. And that is where I first met this wonderful man – Count Stanislaw Kerensky. Stanny. I was captivated. I can see you are thinking, 'Maman, why do I have to listen to your girlish romantic escapades?' But Serge my darling boy, for now please just listen."

She paused for another sip of water, before continuing.

"You know I can still recall that evening so vividly. There was a connection, an instant spark. We had a laugh together, he was an outrageous flirt, but he had such personality you forgave him anything. I remember, suddenly in the middle of the party he grabbed a huge old fur coat, threw it round his shoulders, and with a bottle of champagne in his hand shouted 'On y va! Let's go dancing!'. And that's how it all began, with Ludmilla and me and Maxim and Stanny. For the first time I felt like I belonged, I was part of the set - Stanny made you feel you were a member of the best club in town."

Elodie paused, took another sip of water, and looked directly into Serge's eyes. She was starting to fade, and her voice was weakening.

"There's more to say, much more . . . but it's this damned disease . . . sucks the strength from me . . . I'm so very tired now. Promise me, promise to come back

## LES ANNÉES FOLLES

tomorrow" she whispered.

Serge left the hospital and wandered aimlessly around Argenteuil. In the lobby of the town hall were posters and information reminding visitors of the town's connection with the impressionist painters. Recollecting the images in a book he once owned, he set off for the bridge over the Seine. He peered down into the dark waters of the river - was this the very same bridge made famous by Monet? It was hard to imagine the sailing regattas, the Sunday promenades and the painters setting up their easels on the riverbank. Where once had been vineyards and asparagus fields there were now housing developments. He pictured gentleman sailors relaxing as they steered gently downstream. But the soft white sails made famous by impressionist brushstrokes had long gone; now a scruffy barge motored mid-stream, laden with hidden cargos.

Eventually he found a path by the river and a grassy bank where he sat leaning against an old willow tree, his face turned towards the warmth of weak autumn sunshine. He lit a cigarette and thought more about those paintings and how this place must have changed – perhaps the war, the bombings had taken their toll – and now, instead of the gentle grace of billowing canvas and the creak of oars on wood and leather the river seemed strangely forlorn and it was speeding cars and buses that dominated the skyline. It was the nature of things. It was easy to be nostalgic and to romanticise the past. He only wanted to look to the future, to block out the past. These reflections troubled him. His mother's reminiscences troubled him. What was her secret? Why was she telling him about all these characters from her past? He supposed it was all to do with the effect of the morphine. But even so, why do people dwell in the past? It's either gone, and if it was bad, then *tant pis*, good riddance! And if it was good, then it will feel sad to remember it. So, what's the point?

He returned to see Elodie the next morning, but she was in such a deep, restful sleep that he didn't want to wake her. On the way out of the hospital he spoke to the duty doctor. "How long has she got?" he asked.

"An hour, a day, perhaps a week. No-one can say for sure. She is slipping away, so now it is in the hands of God. She asked for a higher dose of morphine before your visit – she was determined to speak to you."

Serge decided to go into Paris and take lunch with some business associates – anything to avoid the empty passing of time at the hotel. The lunch drifted on into the afternoon and he was late getting back to the hospital in Argenteuil.

In the early evening the last rays of autumn sun had reached across the floor of Elodie's room towards her bed. Almost as soon as Serge entered the room and sat down next to her bed she opened her eyes and looked deep into his.

"I am so very sorry my boy, my Serge. I have not been a good mother and I gave you a bad father."

Serge looked startled – what did this mean?

"A bad father, well that's true. But that's enough of all this talk of Paris in the old days. I went into town today, let me tell you about it. Or, if you like, let me tell you about America - you would love New York!"

But Elodie ignored him, and with a voice so quiet that he had to lean in to hear her she continued, "You don't see the connection, do you? Of course not, why should you? It was a long time ago . . . let me tell you then. The Russian, Count Stanny, the one I told you about . . . I loved him . . . I loved him more than anyone can begin to imagine. He was my earth, my ocean, my sky, my moon and sun. And he loved me, in his way, but he loved everyone too, he loved life like a man possessed. Like a man who is so determined to block out his awful sad memories. He lost his family, he lost his beloved Russia, so he drank, and he spent his money and partied and entertained everyone and became the finest actor he could be, and I swear he played the part better than anyone on any stage. And you realise a man like that cannot truly know the normal love of a man and a woman. Do you understand? But still I loved him despite all his faults and his sadness and I was thrilled to be his girl for a wild, wonderful year in Paris. I suppose I wanted to save him from himself."

"Come closer so you can hear me Serge. You see, the truth is . . . I didn't save him, I failed, and, well, this is the real point of what I must tell you . . . amongst all the gifts he showered on me was one very unexpected present. You see . . . I became pregnant."

Serge's jaw dropped, and his mouth opened, but no words came out. Instead he just took his mother's bony hand in his and watched her.

She was becoming exhausted. The effort had been great. The pain was returning. She gazed at the pale thin strips of sunlight stretching towards her across the tiled floor. She asked for another sip of water, she needed to finish. It was nearly done. She looked into his eyes, the eyes of her son.

"Serge, listen closely. I have never told you because I thought, well, what good would it do, you could never know him, and I have been ashamed, to have a child out of wedlock in those days, well it was a sin. And Henri insisted it was never discussed. But now I feel I was wrong and I should have told you. Serge, I must tell you . . . my lovely boy. . . I have to tell you . . . that Henri, your Papa, was not your true father. Your real father was Stanny. Count Stanislaw Kerensky. In fact, you were christened Sergei, only later we called you Serge. There. I have said it."

As Serge stared into space with astonishment and

disbelief, Elodie reached out her arms to him and he kissed her forehead, and then she sighed a deep sigh and lay back and closed her eyes.

For several minutes Serge stared at the floor, trying to absorb what she had told him. It was truly unbelievable – yet at some deep instinctive level he also knew it was the absolute truth. Something hidden had been revealed, a truth so pure and profound and heart-gladdening he found himself smiling as tears came into his eyes.

He sat by her side for an hour, watching her sleep, holding her hand, brushing her fine hair away from her forehead, letting the cascade of thoughts and emotions wash over him. Eventually he decided that he could not sit and keep a vigil, that he needed air and space to come to terms with what she had told him.

Touching her gently on the shoulder he whispered 'Maman' and instantly she opened her eyes, with a startled look on her face, as if called to some final judgement.

He helped settle her against the pillow and gave her water. He noticed how her skin had a strange tinge of yellow and her eyes were moist and hazy, but also a bright china blue colour, which surprised him, because he remembered them as hazel-grey.

With great effort, Elodie eventually began to speak again, in halting sentences, "I am so tired now, but I must finish. I am so very sorry, my son. Stanny would have been a better father for you. When the baby came he promised to take care of me. But there were many things I didn't know about him. He left us . . . went back to Russia in secret . . . I think he wanted to help old friends . . . and he never came back. It was awful . . . I waited and waited, but nothing. Only this," and she gestured to him to open the drawer of her bedside cupboard. "Inside, look inside."

Serge found an old leather-bound Bible. Tucked inside was a faded postcard. On the front was a hand-coloured image of a flower-seller. It was entitled "Les p'tit métiers de Paris". On the back was a brief message written in a long curling script:

*Elodie, ma Chérie. Forgive me. I would give the world to be with you. But I cannot return. You must go on without me. I adored you. I will never forget. In haste, your Stanny.*

"Listen Maman, this doesn't matter now. Don't trouble yourself, please" said Serge, but still she carried on, in a stuttering whisper, pausing for breath between every sentence.

"Two years later. I was almost destitute. Times were getting hard . . . but I still had my looks, and I met Henri, who became your Papa. He had been divorced but he seemed kind and . . . he had a good position and, well . . . I am sorry, but I grabbed at the opportunity for a better life. I didn't know how he treated you until too late. You were right to run away. You were right to blame me . . . I tried to do the right thing. But life . . ."

Elodie reached out to see the card again. Serge wondered how many times she had looked at this card and read the farewell message over and over. She said, "It is over now. Keep this card Serge . . . Sergei, I want you to have it . . . it is all that we have of your father."

Now the last bout of strength was gone as quickly as it had arrived. She could speak no more words, she slumped against the pillow, lay her head on her side facing Serge, and he saw tears running down the side of her face.

Then, even as Serge's mind struggled with a jumble of confused and conflicting thoughts, he knew that nothing else mattered at that moment other than to find the right words to say, so that his mother would be settled and feel no more remorse and be at peace. All his protective strategies, his obsessive looking forward, all his determination and discipline would count for nothing. He reached over and gently took her face in his hands and to his surprise the words flowed easily. "Maman, I am here with you and that is all that matters. I still care for you so much, despite everything, and I am so sorry I have not been here for you. And you have given me a great gift, telling me about my father, my real father."

"And you know what Maman, let me tell you, I feel

proud to be the son of Count Stanny. In a strange way this all makes sense to me now. Truly, in telling me this you have given me something wonderful that I will treasure all my life. You are not to blame for anything. It is life Maman, just life. Go to sleep now. I will see you tomorrow. I love you."

Elodie closed her eyes and lay still. Her face seemed to relax, and a beatific smile settled briefly across her pale lips. Serge looked at her for some minutes. She appeared to have fallen into an exhausted but peaceful sleep. He got up and went quietly to the window, closing the blind as the dusky light began to fade.

That night, in his hotel, he drank a few glasses of wine in the bar, retired early and slept the longest, deepest sleep of his life, without any dreams.

In the middle of that same night Elodie woke when the nurse came to check on her. Seeing her eyes slowly open, the nurse wiped Elodie's brow and moistened her lips, and then whispered to her. "I saw your son – so handsome! I am so pleased he could be here with you. Rest now Elodie . . . God be with you."

Elodie smiled to herself, perhaps the last smile of her life. Words and thoughts were jumbled in her mind, but peace was what she felt, a deep and soothing peace, caressing her like a gentle sea-breeze, as warm as evening summer sun in the pine-shaded lanes of Fréjus. And there in that lane by the ocean, just ahead of her, silhouetted against the brow of the hill, were those two figures again, a man and a boy, holding hands, walking towards the setting sun.

In the morning, Serge walked to the hospital, stopping to buy a Paris Match magazine and some flowers. The florist was full of chrysanthemums - it was coming up to the Fête des Morts. He remembered Elodie had loved the sunflowers on holiday in the south and he asked the florist, but of course the season had passed. He bought a bouquet of white roses.

As he entered the hospital ward one of the sisters took him quietly to one side. There was no pause, or time to sit down. She simply said, "Monsieur, I am sorry to tell you that your mother passed away during the night. I am so very sorry. She was a lovely woman with a fine spirit and I know it meant everything to her that you visited."

Serge felt utterly shell-shocked. Of course, he knew she was going to die, the way a doctor knows the clinical facts, but he had not had time to feel what it meant, in his mind, in his heart. He stood staring at the sister in complete incomprehension. "But . . . but I saw her just last night. We were going to talk more today. I can't believe it." She sat him down and made him strong sweet tea and let him collect his thoughts.

He declined to see her body. It had been enough to see

her alive one more time, but to see her dead - he couldn't bear it. Overcome with his shock he became aware of an over-whelming aura of sorrow and decay in the building. He needed to get out, to go anywhere. He spoke about funeral arrangements and gave his contact details and left the hospital as quickly as he could. Without really thinking where he was going he boarded a bus into central Paris.

In the city centre he just walked, anywhere, dangling the bouquet of roses from his hand - it felt wrong just to throw them away. He should have given them to the nurse.

After a time, he found himself by the Seine, near the Pont d'Alexandre. He walked across the bridge and leaned over, staring into the ripples and eddies of the fast-flowing river.

One by one he began to throw the white roses down into the current. He watched in fascination as they were caught up so swiftly and transported downstream. Who knows where they might end up, perhaps on the old quay side at Argenteuil, or on the broad white sands of a sunny beach? Or would they simply fall apart, petal by petal, to be washed into oblivion? He supposed it was all a question of belief or faith. Had Elodie, Maman, believed in God? He might never know. But she had believed in him, in her own son, after all. He took the postcard from his jacket pocket and studied it. To give him such a gift, to know the truth about his father!

This was not a bequest of money or the inheritance of some trinket or other. No, this was a truly empowering legacy, a gift with the potential to transform; that is, if he only had the will and the courage to fully accept it, unconditionally, with all his heart and soul.

Beneath the bridge, the river rolled on. Later that year he changed his name to Sergei.

# *Waiting*

## April 1997

On a warm Sunday afternoon in spring, just a stone's throw from the Jardin des Tuileries, Didier Lelouche found himself standing near the Métro entrance, a bunch of flowers in one hand, an envelope and a postcard in the other, an honest man compromised by his dreams, on the edge of the second most important decision of his life.

He was short and wiry, with warm, melancholic eyes and a nest of thick unruly black hair. At the age of thirty, in order to try to look a little more like Omar Sharif, who was the movie idol of his mother-in-law, he had grown a moustache. The coarse hair sprouted vigorously from his swarthy skin across his top lip and down the sides of his mouth so that in appearance he resembled the unhappy faces that young children draw with crayons, where the smile is turned upside down. Although no-one volunteered to tell him that he still did not look like Omar Sharif, nevertheless there was an unexpectedly positive side-effect at his work, where the restaurant clientele found that his easy smile and pleasant manner created a charming counter-point to the somewhat comical moustache and the rather mournful eyes.

Didier's childhood was spent in the sleepy hamlets and farms of the ancient Province of Berry where the seasons changed but the locals didn't. Since coming to Paris to seek his fortune he had noticed the opposite effect – not so much in the way of seasons, but the inhabitants were constantly moving on and reinventing themselves. In the *banlieue defavorisée* where he first lived he encountered a travelling circus of nationalities and races; some troubled, some happy, but always seeking a better life. And where he waited tables in the prestigious *1er arrondissement* it was an ever-shifting tableau of faces – star-struck tourists from far away continents, bejewelled Parisians playing with their new mobile phones and minor celebrities whose names he did not recognise.

Growing up in the gentle, quiet rooms of his family farmhouse in the country had given him a calm open-eyed outlook. Life in the remote villages was often a challenge to man and beast. But even when the most biblical storms damaged their crops or when the ewes gave birth to dead or inauspiciously deformed lambs he witnessed his father's brow remain untroubled and his shoulders stay broad and strong, so the young boy wished to emulate and please his father. There was no doubt that he would have stayed on the farm, his Papa's dearest wish, were it not for the foreign seed planted within him at an early age by his mother.

For it was Maman who had given him the magazines and illustrated books which opened his eyes to the wider world and it was she who had taken him one day on the long train journey to Paris where he stared in astonishment at the Eiffel Tower in all its triumphant mechanical glory and was bewitched by the spot-lit chanteuses his mother adored. For although she accepted her duties as a farmer's wife with fortitude and patience, when the chores were done she would take off her housecoat, put on a patterned dress, dab a little perfume next to the bright scarf at her neck and switch on the radio. Then, while Papa was still in the barn or on the tractor, it was just she and Didier alone in the kitchen. She would sing along to the tunes and reach out her long arms to the young boy, twirling him around the stone floor until his head was spinning. "Always believe in yourself Didier and you can reach the stars" was a mantra she whispered, not appreciating how with these words she had breathed life into a tiny restless worm of ambition that would wriggle uncomfortably in his soul until the day he would have it out once and for all. She had parted the veil and he had glimpsed a world of glimmering and exotic possibilities which lay beyond the rough gates of the farm. In the years that followed, Didier would sit alone in his room, diligently finishing his devoirs, but always glancing up at the cork board on the wall where were pinned the Paris postcards, the tickets from the Métro, the programme from the Piaf concert and the little map of the city, creased where he and Maman had opened and closed it a thousand times as they traversed the boulevards. Like the tokens that adorn a shrine, these precious keepsakes would always remind him of Maman. She, having passed the baton of her youthful aspirations on to him, was unable to nurture her hopes for the boy because the onset of a virulent breast cancer took her life at the age of just thirty-eight.

For four more years after the premature death of his mother Didier and his father pressed on through the hot summers and freezing winters, the boy loyally helping his Papa with the chores before settling down to do his homework. Sundays had always meant a visit to his grandparents, André and Emilie, and Grandpa would teach him how to play chess or tell fantastical stories of Paris when he was a young man and grandma Emilie would sigh and tut. Didier began to see where his mother's yearning for Paris came from. One day, it was the year Grandma Emilie passed, he and Papi visited the village cemetery to lay chrysanthemums during the Fête des Morts. As they walked away, passing the cypress trees at the entrance, André took the boys hand and whispered something that shocked him: "Get out of this place Didi, see the world, go to Paris!"

The bond of respect and unspoken love between father and son remained unbroken by his mother's early passing. But they dared not acknowledge that some joy had evaporated, some hidden rhythm was lost and to Didier the days began to play out a repetitive and monotonous tune. He began to crave variety and to dream of a life where he could labour to a different beat. He was no great academic at school but still he revised late into the night and despite his father's lack of interest, he managed a place at catering school in Orléans. One autumn day, having just turned sixteen, he found himself standing at the farm gate, with a backpack and a case with his books, looking into the grieving watery eyes and weather-lined face of his ageing father, knowing that he would have to do something to make his father proud.

By committing conscientiously to his hotel training he discovered to his delight that he could be adept and capable of much more than farming and reading. And because his memories of Paris with Maman were deep-rooted within him, he knew that he would be unable to resist the siren call when it came. Yet when the opportunity arose to quit the provinces it proved tougher than he could have imagined.

Arriving in the great city of his dreams he was forced to take one poorly paid waiting job after another, to share one cheap run-down apartment after another. After a year of frustration and restless meandering he feared his mind was becoming lost in a maelstrom of endless uncertainty. His ambition remained caged within him, embryonic and unformed.

And yet, just when he feared his soul was beginning to shrivel and his mind was dwelling more and more on a possible return to the country; just when he had begun to think that he would never again feel the sense of peace and stability he had known as a child, something unexpected happened that pleasantly interrupted the joyless and frenetic pattern of his life in Paris.

In a Lebanese café near St Ouen he had looked up from his phone one day and stared, a little longer than was polite, into the mysterious, soft eyes of a striking young woman who was clearing his table. Soon he found himself returning before and after his shifts to sit in the far corner of that same café slowly drinking petite tasse after petite tasse while glancing surreptitiously at this Levantine beauty. He observed the graceful choreography of her movements, the way her slender arm moved in circles as she wiped the zinc bar, the precise angle of her back as she leaned to clear the plates, the slight swaying of her hips as she weaved among the tables on her way from the kitchen and the quiet enigmatic smile on her lips as she spoke to clients and took orders. He drank in detail after detail: those beguiling, almond shaped eyes, the extraordinary smoothness of her olive skin, the loose strands of glossy black hair escaping from her headscarf and the subtle scent of jasmine oil as she brought him another coffee that his already racing heart could not endure.

He soon learned that her name was Amina and she was in fact not Lebanese but Egyptian, a Coptic Christian. For Didier it mattered not – she was simply the most graceful and magical figure of a woman that he could have ever imagined – so different from the red-cheeked country-girls of his youth. With a drive and ambition that surprised himself, he set out to know her and to win her heart.

So it was, that amidst the seeming hopelessness of his early years in Paris, Amina became not only his girlfriend and, six months later, his cherished wife, but also his precious lodestar, the centre-point to which he could return when the challenges and frustrations of his work became too much or when the sheer craziness of the city stretched the sinews of his mind to snapping point. Her gentle shy smile, the way she loved him and seemed to know his soul, the way her mother and brothers allowed him into their humble yet exotic lives in Paris with its respect for the traditions of their

Egyptian homeland, so many miles away. With this newfound equilibrium in his life, the years began to glide along more quickly, calmly at first but then at a frightening pace especially after their first child Lilli arrived.

Sometime after the milestone of his thirtieth birthday Didier began to sense a turbulence within himself, a stirring of long-forgotten identity. A visit to his father had shocked him – the old man was still struggling on with limited help. He wanted to send more money, to show his Papa how well he was doing, that he had made the right decision. He saw friends and neighbours moving up and moving on – it made him unsettled – and the graceless flower of ambition began to bud within his heart.

He became impatient and frustrated with the restaurant where he worked. He was a senior waiter, but the limited scope of the role could no longer contain the scale of his hopes and dreams. His mind became fixated on the idea of opening a restaurant and although he knew Amina was frightened by the idea, nevertheless it began to obsess him and he spent more and more time scheming and planning on his own, viewing premises, meeting chefs, secretly putting money aside, making promises he might not be able to keep, all the while imagining that one day he would reveal his creation to Amina, to her family and to his father, and to all his friends who would be astonished and impressed – it would be a defining moment.

In this strange way Didier's plan became a secret obsession and he pursued it with unhealthy zeal, polishing it in his mind and treasuring it only for himself like a child with a stolen toy, not realising that he had excluded the people who cared most for him and least for his ambition. He pursued this private obsession until, inevitably, the moment came when things would have to become real. He knew there would be a junction, a turning point, after which there could be no turning back. It came one warm Sunday in April and he thought he was ready for it.

Didier liked working on Sundays. He wasn't due in until eleven and there was no alarm clock to wake him from his dreams. He liked to stretch alongside Amina and run his hands over the taught smooth skin of her belly. Five months now. Much as he adored his little daughter Lilli he secretly hoped for a boy this time. But whether boy or girl he knew the child would be both a joy and a financial burden, and the extra responsibility troubled him, especially if it might compromise his dreams for the restaurant. But that worry could wait; now it was Sunday morning and there was time for a leisurely breakfast. Amina prepared ful medames the traditional Egyptian way, but the child was allowed Nutella on toast. Didier ate both.

This day was special; he had a blueprint, a purpose that

he had first conceived many months before. After a bright dawn the sun was casting dark shadows from the concrete towers of the périphérique as he skirted the St Ouen flea markets. Ivorian and Senegalese street vendors were setting up for the day with their bright fabrics laid on the ground, selling lurid jewellery and carved wooden figurines, and always with a boom box playing Afro funk. Across the road he shouted "Salut Régis!" to the boulanger who would put aside a loaf for him to pick up later. In the markets he knew the vendors would be laying out their stalls ready to sell a cornucopia of bijoux, trinkets, antiquités and all manner of vintage paraphernalia which he couldn't afford and didn't want anyway. Instead he headed straight for the Métro Garibaldi. In the sunshine everybody seemed happy. He took it as another sign.

At that time of day, the Métro carriage was quiet. You couldn't begin to compare it with the stifling crush of a week-day. It was only a half dozen stops, but on a week-day it seemed to Didier like the whole world was headed across town or changing for onward destinations at Gare Montparnasse. Ten years in Paris and yet for a country boy he never could get used to the sheer mass of humanity on the move in the city and he still dreamed of the quiet lanes and wide horizons of his boyhood.

As the train rolled out of Garibaldi he reached into his

jacket pocket and made sure the envelope was still there. This would be the day, he'd made up his mind, and today he intended to say au revoir to the routines of waiting on tables and bonjour to his new life as entrepreneur and restaurateur. He'd found a cute little café, ripe for conversion. The location was good, just on the edge of Batignolles. He'd done his research and he was confident of attracting some of the monied bobos with a southern Mediterranean fusion menu. He had a talented cook lined up, ready to go, and he would handle front of house and hire young locals to help in the kitchens. The only niggling dent in his polished plan, a fact that he tried to ignore, was that he hadn't told Amina – because he knew that with the baby on the way she would be too cautious. But he told himself she would come around once she saw the cash rolling in and the happy faces of diners. She would support him, of course she would, but his love for her was deep and he feared her reaction to this fait accomplis. But this dream had been a long time in the nurturing. What did his mother use to say? 'Just believe in yourself Didier and the world will be yours'.

His thoughts ran on. Who could blame him for having ambition? Wasn't that what the city was fuelled by? When his Maman was taken so early, so cruelly, he had stayed on and paid his dues hadn't he? And she would surely have been proud of him, striking out for the city she had shown him as a boy, seeking the world and his place in it? And it was typical of Papa that he whispered doubts into the boy's ear and placed the key to the farm-house in his palm. 'This is your home and your heritage Didier, don't abandon it for a folly'. But it wasn't enough - he would show the old man how wrong he was.

Exiting at Concorde Métro, Didier strode the familiar path to his workplace, passing in front of the imposing carved doors and the plate glass windows of the restaurant, around the corner and down an alley where a steel door opened into the delivery bay and the back entrance.

The Restaurant Normandie stood proudly on the corner of the Marché Saint-Honoré, a stone's throw from the glitz and upscale brands of the Place Vendôme. Back in the 30's the wealthy founders had been so impressed by their inaugural passage to New York on the SS Normandie that they designed their new dining hall as an homage to the stylish and swift ocean liner.

There was no denying its charm and ambiance. Didier still enjoyed the atmosphere. How could you not? The clients would regularly comment on the majestic art deco mirrors, the panels with exquisite mosaics of scenes from the thirties: the Normandie departing from Le Havre, a glamorous girl waving to the crowds on the docks. The bar itself ran the length of the restaurant - a polished bulwark of dark teak and brass. With its aura of nostalgia and faded glamour, to dine at the Normandie was more like a theatrical experience. The white linen table cloths, enormous leather-bound menus and gleaming silver cutlery formed essential elements of the stage set. Suited and booted, bow ties and shining shoes, highly trained, attentive, efficient and elegant were the cast of chefs, waiters, sommeliers and receptionists who presented this culinary performance, twice a day, six days a week.

And Didier played his part – he'd waited tables at the Normandie for five years now. After training at the Hôtel Ecolier he'd apprenticed in some rough kitchens and fancy bistros to work his way up. He was proud of his knowledge and his skills. He knew the boats that brought in the Bretagne lobsters and the Périgord farms where the foie gras was farmed. He knew Escoffier's five 'mother' sauces and he knew which chefs were on the way up or down the starry Michelin staircase. But most of all he served his guests with calm detachment and expertise, with pride yet without haughtiness (he knew what the world thinks of Parisians). He delivered both charm and professionalism, and, when called upon to engage in conversation with his diners he could show empathy and wit while remaining respectful. Because one *must* respect the ritual of the meal. To sit and eat with family, with friends, with a business partner or with a loved one – this is the ritual that must be respected. And a meal at the Normandie was always a special occasion. No doubt that in the hip bars and bistros of the Canal St Martin or in the Marais things were more relaxed and informal, but here in the premiere arrondissement to be a waiter in the Normandie was a serious and noble profession. Didier had learned all this and more, but now compared to the intoxicating dream of his own restaurant, how could it be enough?

With his efficiency, his diligence and attentive way with the clientele it wasn't too long before Didier made it to senior waiter, but he could see no progression beyond that level. The imposing figure of Jacques Matolle, Maitre D'hôtel of the Normandie for the last thirty-three years, stood solidly between him and further advancement. Jacques was a veteran, an unimpeachable figurehead of the culinary establishment.

In the changing room he switched into his uniform; crisp white shirt, black bow tie, black trousers and waistcoat, starched white apron and highly polished black leather shoes. He wondered whether to take his envelope with him but decided to leave it unfolded in his jacket. Greeting Jacques at the bar, he looked to see who was on the Sunday shift with him and took a quick scan of the bookings. Gilles, Marty, Jacques and the new girl Sylvie would cover the tables. Seventy booked plus walk-ins. Not a problem. Jacques asked him to look after the front section including two tables of eight in the window seats.

By midday the clients started to arrive and just as things started to get busy Didier suddenly remembered this was no normal Sunday – he was so accustomed to the slick routine that he had temporarily forgotten the significance of the day. Glancing over at Jacques, standing imperiously at his lectern, greeting clients with his masterful bonhomie, he wandered whether he could really do it – have the conversation and tell Jacques that he was leaving. Conscious that his palms were sweating and his heart pounding a little faster he ducked into the men's room and splashed his face with cold water. Looking in the mirror, he straightened his tie, ran a comb through his thick black hair and said to himself 'Come on Didier, you can do it. Believe in yourself. It's for you. It's for Amina and Lilli and Maman. One last time then it's over. Let's make it a good one'.

Didier re-entered the main room as one of the two window tables arrived. With a practiced eye and ear, he observed them: a Parisian family, well-spoken, three generations, probably driven over from a big apartment in the 6th, summer at a family farm or a manoir in the country. But while he made these shrewd private observations, still he made them without condescension because if you were serious you learned early on to treat all clients with the same respect regardless of social milieu – they are paying your wages. He gave them their menus, took their orders for aperitifs and was suitably endearing to the two kids who wanted Coke, but Papa said not today, and so Didier said if they were good he would ask chef to create a special drink made in the kitchen just for les petites. They had class this family, you could tell. The father wore an expensive sports jacket and a tailored shirt and Didier noticed the fine Swiss watch on a leather strap at the edge of his cuff. Mother was attractive in an expensive looking silk shirt and pearls and even grand-mere looked elegant in a tweedy jacket with a glittery diamante leopard brooch on the lapel. As he came to take orders they asked him earnestly about the fish of the day, about the way the veal was cooked, where did they get their artichokes from, and so on. He enjoyed helping them with their decisions, making little suggestions all the while listening to their family chatter and laughter - they were charming this family, he thought.

They wanted to know about the oysters, were they from Marennes? And where did the veal come from? "From near Bourges in the Berry, Monsieur" he replied, "I know it well". Even as he said it, he knew he had broken a house rule and volunteered that little snippet of personal information without being asked. He thought they might recoil but it only spurred them on to ask more about the region, did he grow up there, how they loved the Loire valley and summers in the countryside. After some jolly discussion they all decided on their entrées and main plats and Didier was about to return to the pass when the father said, "I think we'll have the Sancerre with the entrées but for main course perhaps you would care to recommend a wine from your region – surprise us!" Didier thanked the father and explained with great courtesy that the Sommelier would arrive shortly to take their wine order and he was sure he would find just the right combination. But with a warm smile, the father said "Well, just this once shall we break the rules and you can suggest one bottle for me and the sommelier can take care of the rest. Something for my wife and her mother, they are having the sole." Confounded by this turn of events Didier paused for a moment and then remembered it was his last day so he thought 'well, why not, Antoine will be furious but who cares, the client comes first'.

"Well, Monsieur, if you insist. Permit me to suggest as an accompaniment to the sole, a Bourgeuil; as you will of course be aware it is a Loire wine made with Cabernet Franc and it should be served a little chilled. This would be ideal with the sole, in my opinion." Didier replied.

The father raised his eyebrows and glanced across at his mother-in-law for approval which he obtained with a raised eyebrow from the end of the table. "Let's have it!" he said to

Didier.

Didier knew this tiny incident would cause a flare up later, but he was too pre-occupied attending to the other large table in the window to worry about it for now. They had hardly sat down when one of these new arrivals barked at him "Cristal champagne pour tous!" It took Didier a few milliseconds to realise he had a party of eight Russians to look after. As he brought champagne flutes and placed them discreetly on the table it gave him the opportunity to glance surreptitiously at their immaculately tailored designer jeans, the men with expensive leather jackets, the girls with enough Louis Vuitton and Prada between them to start a small boutique. Didier wondered why they wanted Cristal when he could have told them of ten other champagnes that were cheaper and better. As they came to order it was the same routine – they ordered the most expensive items from the menu, oysters, foie gras, steak tartare, chateaubriand steaks, lobster Mornay – all the finest classics. In Didier's experience the Americans and British asked lots of questions about the menu, but seldom got into a discussion, whereas the French would of course cheerfully enter into a little debate about which dish to have or about the provenance of the food. Now with these Russians it was bang, food ordered and let's tuck into the Cristal - but they were a jovial bunch for all that, getting louder with each sip of champagne.

With all his initial orders placed and the wine and drinks under control Didier paused for a moment near the bar, scanning the room instinctively, making sure everything was running smoothly. Just then, Antoine the sommelier grabbed him by the elbow and marched him into the corridor "What the hell are you playing at giving them advice about wine?! That's my job and I've been in it for twenty years, so I think you ought to show more respect!" he barked.

"But the father asked me personally! He insisted, so what could I do?" replied Didier, pushing Antoine's hand off his elbow.

"No way! You always refer to the sommelier. I shall see what Jacques thinks about this later!"

For a few seconds, this conversation let loose an angry bee in Didier's mind.

'Later?' he thought 'yes, you go right ahead because *later* is when I won't even be here so who cares, you pretentious buffoon. And as for Jacques, the grand Maître de bullshit, it won't matter a fig what he thinks either 'cos he will be looking for someone else to boss about!'

He reflected that the most annoying thing about Jacques was simply the fact that he was *always* there, an unflappable front of house presence, *always* right about everything, running a tight ship to please the owners, sweet-talking the regulars, charming the tourists, cracking the whip with the waiters and twisting the chef's arm to produce the goods time and time again.

But there was no time for resentment on a busy Sunday lunch-time shift, so Didier was back into action within seconds, delivering plate after plate with grace and aplomb, attending to every query and request with the panache and poise of a ballroom dancer. The service was soon in full flow, the Parisians convivial and appreciative of the freshest sea-food, the children enjoying the chef's special *boisson* and grand-mere telling them a story as she quaffed a large glass of Sancerre. Later, he couldn't help but notice the bottle of Bourgueil beside the table and made a point of asking Madame how she enjoyed her sole but although she was complimentary about the fish she said nothing about the wine, which worried him a little. But still he loved this French family, their civility, their manners, their bearing – they were the perfect diners for the Normandie – he could wait on people like this all day.

By contrast on the Russian table the men had gathered at one end of the table and were deep in animated conversation, knocking back large glasses of Chateau Cheval Blanc as they tore into their steaks while three of the girls chatted or looked at their phones, picking at their food. The fourth girl was absent. He made a point of asking if all was well with their food and the older guy slapped him on the back and said "Super bon – absolument!" It was easy to judge, they were crude for sure, but they were honest – they had money and they wanted the best. It was his job at that moment simply to deliver whatever they wanted.

A strange thing happened. At the back of the restaurant, in a corridor near the toilets, he recognised one of the girls from the Russian table. As he stepped back to let her pass she stopped and in perfect French asked him if he would do her a little favour? At which point she rather hastily reached into her handbag and handed him a postcard. "I need to send this, it's important, but silly me I don't have any stamps. Would you do me a big favour and put a stamp on it and put it in a box for me?" she said.

She had rather wonderful eyes and a delightful perfume, and she was standing quite close to Didier. It didn't occur to him for a single moment to ask why she couldn't post it herself. Trained to do whatever the customer asks he simply said, "Of course Mademoiselle, no problem", and put the card into his pocket.

As desserts gave way to coffee and the presentation of the bills, so the first guests started to leave, and the restaurant gradually quietened. Didier liked this moment, because you could see the end of another successful shift, you could sense the mood of people as they left, full of good food, happy from the wine and the art of conversation. For all the finery of the menu he knew it all came down to making people happy with simple things: good food, conversation, a little wine. He knew this simple formula would serve him well in his new venture. He stood at the end of the bar and looked around the majestic dining hall once more – what a place – how he would miss it!

The Parisian family were leaving, and he helped them with their coats, noticing the fine wool of grand-mère's cashmere coat and the aroma of expensive leather coming from Father's jacket. As he wished them a *'bonne fin de journée'* he returned to the table to clear the remaining coffee cups. Out of the corner of his eye he noticed the Father was lingering by the door in conversation with Jacques who was ushering them out of the entrance with his inimitable charm.

With most of the other diners having left to enjoy a Sunday afternoon stroll in the warming April sun only the Russian table remained. The men were now huddled together in more earnest conversation cradling Armagnacs while the four girls were beginning to send impatient signals down to the other end of the table. Eventually the girls won, the bill was called for and Didier was not surprised to see the total of over two thousand Euros – Jacques would be pleased to see that tidy little contribution to the coffers.

As Didier dealt with coats and wished them a pleasant

afternoon the tall, square-jawed man who seemed to be the party leader came over to Didier with a broad smile and an outstretched hand. It wasn't the custom to shake hands with the customers unless you knew them well, but you had to make allowances for different nationalities, so Didier shook his hand. As he did so he could feel some small object within the man's strong hand, touching his palm. As a younger man he would have immediately looked at it and drawn unnecessary attention but there was a look in the man's eyes which told him this was deliberate, and he should not draw attention to it, so he slipped it into his trouser pocket without looking. Within seconds they were all on their way out, with Gilles, Antoine and Didier all taking a moment to bid their most charming adieus to the pretty Russian girls.

A few minutes later, Didier popped into the staff toilet, sat down in the cubicle and fished the mysterious folded paper note out of his pocket, somehow expecting to read a cryptic message. But to his amazement the paper in his hand was clearly a euro bank note and as he unfolded it he saw the number '5' and guessed it was a fifty euro note but then it was pink and fifty-euro notes were brown. With his jaw dropping Didier found himself staring at the rare yet unmistakeable pink-purple colour of a five hundred euro note.

He was utterly dumb-founded - the biggest tip he had ever heard of in the restaurant was a hundred Euros and here he was staring at almost a week's wages and a sum that would buy valuable equipment for his new business. He went back into the restaurant to help clearing down the tables yet within moments his conscience started to trouble him, and he imagined that he felt banknote pressing hotly against his thigh from inside his trouser pocket. The dilemma was that all tips were supposed to go into the Maître d'hôtel's tip box for sharing with the kitchen. But he thought to himself that this money had been deliberately handed direct to him and not left on the table, as if the Russian wanted him to have it himself, as if they knew he needed it. Perhaps it was a sign?

He was distracted now, and it must have become obvious to others because just then the new girl Sylvie glided past him and gave him a friendly pat on the back. "Ca va Didier?" she enquired.

A moment later his mind was thrown into even more turmoil as Jacques appeared from his office and with an authoritative hand gesture summoned him for a chat. This only happened when there was some miniscule error during service that had not escaped the Maître d's discerning eye and a sharp reprimand usually followed. In Didier's guilty thoughts he was already having to apologise for over-stepping the mark with his wine recommendations or worse still having to confess to serious underhand behaviour for keeping tips to himself. Either way it was going to be bad, so he figured he'd better grab his resignation letter from his day coat and bring it with him. At least for once he would have the surprise hand to play.

Jacques's office was a gloomy, dark wood-panelled box which had once been a store room – it had just one window throwing in a little daylight. As Didier sat down opposite Jacques's desk he shot a wistful glance at the tiny square of blue sky that could just be seen from that window.

To his surprise Jacques reached into a cupboard behind the desk and retrieved two glasses and a bottle of cognac. Without asking Didier he poured a couple of shots and pushed the old crystal brandy goblets across the desk. This was clearly very bad news thought Didier if he's having to soften me up first, but it's Jacques who's going to need a drop most when I give him my letter.

Jacques leaned back, warming the brandy with the glass in his hands. "Didier" he said, "it's time we had a conversation. It's been on my mind for some time and after today, well something tells me we should talk – no time like the present eh?"

Didier sat slightly hunched, conscious of his envelope poking out of the pocket of his waistcoat while he shuffled to get comfortable and sipped at the strong liquor. Bad news was coming - maybe he should get his news in first?

But Jacques continued before Didier had a chance to interject.

"It's been five years now hasn't it and apart from a few early difficulties it has been a pleasure working with you. I have watched you fine-tune your skills, you are always in command of the situation, always polite and helpful, always attentive and efficient and you are liked by all the staff. Today with that family, the table at the window, that was you at your very best."

Didier was flabbergasted by what he was hearing. "But what about Antoine and the wine?" he responded.

"Ah the wine, yes indeed. Antoine made a complaint, of course he did. As you know a sommelier is proud of his status and his knowledge, but if I have learned one thing it is that the customer comes first, and certainly comes before the sommelier's ego. So, let me share with you what the father of that family said to me as he left. He not only complimented us for the food and the service and promised to return, but he made a point of complimenting you for your attention to his family and his children but especially for recommending the chilled Bourgueil which his wife and mother had described as a revelation."

Didier was speechless. His mood began to shift from resignation to shock – he couldn't quite believe what he was hearing.

"And this is what pleases me most," Jacques continued, "that you are not afraid to take charge of the situation and be creative with the customer."

He paused for a few seconds and sipped at his brandy, then continued.

"Now you must realise I am going to have to retire soon? No? Well perhaps I hide it well, so I'll share the truth with you now. Not only am I sixty-two years old and getting a little tired of this but also this last year has been harder as I have a small medical problem, nothing terrible but it slows me up. Madame Lafarge is rightly concerned should anything happen to me or they worry that I cannot cope, so they have been asking me to consider my successor. I feel that I should do something about it while I can still be here to help a new person settle in and take command. So, Didier, although you are young, still I was also young when I first became Maître d'hôtel and I think we can work together to have a successful handover during this coming year. You look shocked – did this not occur to you as a possibility?"

Didier sat looking blankly at Jacques, wondering if he had heard it all correctly.

"So, let me please clarify this – are you saying that you want me to take over your position and this has been approved by the owners?"

"Indeed, that is exactly what I am saying. I must say I

thought you would have reacted a little more positively?"

Didier began to wonder what kind of strange, surreal Sunday he was having. First the extraordinary five hundred Euro tip, then the offer of a huge promotion, all on the same day he was due to hand in his notice. He imagined telling Amina about this, how they would laugh out of sheer amazement, how he would be able to tell his father.

He tried to gather his thoughts. "No, I mean, yes" he said, "I really appreciate this, I mean, enormously, and I just hadn't expected this. I am very grateful, err . . . please allow me a few days to reflect on this?"

"Of course, of course you will want to discuss with your wife, which is natural. Now what is the other matter you wanted to discuss?"

"Other matter?" queried Didier

"Yes" said Jacques, "the matter that is contained in the envelope which is protruding so importantly from your pocket!"

Didier grasped the envelope and turned it over in his hand. The contents of that letter had been a long time in the planning, he reflected, and he had been determined to hand it in today, he had imagined and played over the conversation in his mind a hundred times. Yet now it sat in his hand like a guilty secret and he stumbled out a brief explanation.

"Oh, it's nothing, just a letter I have to post."

## WAITING

"On Sunday?" said Jacques, with a quizzical and mischievous glint in his eye. But with that he rose from his desk and ushered Didier out of his office with an arm around his shoulder.

"Listen Didier, you have done well today and it's going to be quiet this evening, so go home early and think this all over and we can talk again tomorrow, yes? *À demain mon collègue!*"

Dazed to the point of bewilderment, Didier changed from his uniform into his casual clothes and stepped blinking into the still bright sunshine of the spring day, still reeling from the astonishing conversation with Jacques.

Without being conscious of where he was going he found himself on the Rue de Rivoli at the iron gates leading into the Jardins des Tuileries. He needed time to collect his thoughts, so he entered the park and joined the locals and tourists strolling among the massed banks of tulips swaying gently in the light breeze of a warm spring afternoon. He sat down on a chair and watched the P'tits Voiliers, the little wooden sailboats dipping their bows and heading purposefully for the opposite side of the Grand Bassin where the children waited with excitement. Life was so perplexing. What kind of voyage was he on and who was in control? Who could navigate the course of their own lives the way these toy yachts allowed the breeze to lift them confidently on their way? Perhaps you just had to be patient with life and wait? He thought about his mother and how she talked about reaching the stars, and he wanted so badly to reach them for her. He noticed the simple delight on the children's faces as their little boats set sail. The clouds were reflected in the water. 'Maybe the stars are right here among us', he thought, 'and perhaps my dreams and hopes are mere reflections?' He got up and placed his hands in the water, just to feel the cooling sensation and to watch the clouds disappear under the ripples.

With these thoughts spinning in his mind, he meandered through the gardens and found himself at the Place de la Concorde. He watched families coming in and out of the Tuileries, children laughing, tourists smiling and taking photos to share with loved ones and suddenly and overwhelmingly it all became too much for him and tears came to his eyes and he turned his face away from the crowds and let the tears fall. He thought of Amina and Lilli - how they were the very best things in his life and he had them already, for free, with no price to pay and no fighting ambition needed to reach them - they were already there, his heaven on earth. He could be home early and surprise them, so, wiping his face, he headed for the Concorde Métro. Still he thought of the conversation with Jacques – with disbelief but with a growing sense of pride - perhaps life was finally going to grant him something to be proud of, something to tell his Papa.

Across the street he stopped to buy an enormous bouquet of tulips for Amina and as his hand went into his coat for his wallet he saw again the pink five hundred euro note and he just laughed out loud – what kind of crazy world is this!? He would ask Amina what to do with the money, she would be his guide. As he placed his wallet back he felt the stiff paper edge of the envelope containing his letter of resignation and next to it, the postcard given to him by the Russian girl – he had completely forgotten that! What a strange day.

The card showed a painting by Manet. He recognised it - the girl at the bar of Folies Bergère, with her wistful, enigmatic look. And in the reflection of the mirror a man is staring at her, expressionless. Is the man her lover, or does he have power over her in some way? Taking a stamp from his wallet, Didier turned the card over and stuck the stamp on the corner. Who would not want to look at what she had written? It came as such a shock, to read the scribbled words that allowed a stranger to peer into someone else's intimate world, to have their pain and fear exposed. What terrible trauma was she suffering? What were his worries in this life compared to others? She must have been so scared to be unable to post this card herself. Perhaps she was controlled by the same man who gave him the huge tip? Didier saw her face again in his mind and he felt ashamed to have read the card. Feeling awkward, as if afraid of being caught peeping into someone else's private life, he quickly found a post-box and despatched the card on its fateful journey.

He walked back to the Métro and stood next to the entrance, as if frozen. Perhaps fate was not always fickle, perhaps we are given a chance here and there to decide our destinies, to have a throw of the dice? He stared at the plain white envelope in his hand, knowing full well that it represented all that he had invested in his precious plans and his secret pride. What would it mean to abandon it all now? What kind of man would it make him, to have nurtured a dream worthy of his mother's ambition, to have pursued it with a burning determination and then to abandon it like a shame-faced child, on a simple twist of fate?

He looked up at the flickering sunlight dancing in the fresh new leaves of the tall plane trees. He took a deep breath, inhaling to fill his lungs. Maman would love to be here with me now in Paris, he thought.

What was it that made him change his mind? Was it walking in the park, watching the boats, seeing the people of Paris at their simple leisure on a Sunday afternoon? Was it the shock of reading the postcard? The extraordinary tip? The unexpected offer of promotion? Was it shedding those tears that cleared his mind and gave him a renewed sense of certainty and peace within himself?

Didier Lelouche would never be sure. But he knew, as his Papa used to say, that sometimes just to take a decision, any decision, is the best course of action. He dropped the envelope in a litter bin, walked briskly down the steps into the Métro, clutching the tulips and smiling to himself.

# Russian Doll

## June 1997

"Jules!" I said, "What on earth are you doing in this fleapit?!"

"Shhh!" he said in a rather theatrical whisper, "How did you find me?"

"I didn't *find* you. This is my local and you appear to be hiding in it! What's going on?"

"I can't tell you, not right now. I've been a bloody fool George," replied Jules.

I suppose I should give you a bit of background. You see, I like to change my watering holes in Paris every few years. It's good for the soul. Bar owners come and go, or they get some fancy notion to refresh the decor in the vain hope of attracting hipper clientele, presumably saying au revoir to the likes of me. They start stripping out the old wooden bars and installing fancy lighting and soon enough my regular seat has been replaced by a chrome bar stool or one of those environmentally disastrous patio warmers. That's my cue to bid adieu and move on. When men with oiled beards and vintage plimsolls start ordering avocado on toast I'm on my bike and heading for seedier haunts more suited to a wizened journo.

But not Jules. Au contraire. Jules survives off any lingering scraps of minor celebrity stardom that he can scrounge. I saw him, I suppose it must be six months ago, at the tables outside Olivier's Café in the Canal St Martin, holding court with a cluster of impressionable wannabe conceptual artists and scribblers. Wavy, greying, yet remarkably shiny hair dragged back behind his ears, that ridiculous gold stud earring and a permanently lit fag creating a light smoky haze through which he contrived to gaze inscrutably at his acolytes. And they lapped him up. Jules Moncrieff, the born-again modernist poet who bore just enough resemblance to Leonard Cohen to be considered a 'cool older guy'. You had to hand it to him, he knew how to perform in front of those wide-eyed arriviste hipsters from Stockholm and Sydney and God knows where else. To them he appeared intriguing and authentic, they saw him as part of a much earlier, de-sanitised Paris – a city of fermenting revolution, of avant-garde artists, boulevard romances and experimental encounters in attic rooms.

Anyway, the other day I popped in to Café Lautrec, my

preferred drinkery de jour. It's rather a tatty estaminet but apart from some tired Belle Epoque prints on the walls it is pleasingly unpretentious, which is how I like it. I ordered my usual noisette with a Cognac chaser and settled down with Le Figaro when I noticed something slightly unusual. There's a table at the rear of the bar, just in front of the door to the courtyard to which us smokers are miserably banished these days. The table is always empty, but not that day. Someone was sitting there, but they were obscured by the trivial antics of some ghastly football team or other - a copy of L'Equipe newspaper held up like a screen in front of them. I sniffed a bit of mystery - it just had that sense of someone deliberately hiding behind the paper – like a badly directed spy movie. I didn't pay it any more attention until I went out for a fag and as I passed the table the mysterious secret agent behind the newspaper turned a page and I caught a glimpse of an unmistakable profile - blow me if it wasn't Jules!

Where was I? Oh yes, so he said he'd been a fool and couldn't tell me why. "Can't tell me??!" I said with astonishment.

I ought to tell you that I've been in Paris now for twenty odd years and although Jules is not exactly top of my soirée invite list, mainly because he tells such whopping lies and gets objectionably drunk; even so we count each other as old muggers and I've seen him through his highs and lows. In fact, I've picked him up and pieced him back together on more than a few occasions. He's a garrulous chap at the best of times but when he's had a few you just can't stop him. So, what the hell was he playing at now and what on earth could he *not* tell me?

He looked bloody awful, his eyes were bloodshot, and a pair of yellow-grey bags sagged loosely under each eye as if Picasso had personally arranged them. It was obvious he hadn't slept in weeks and he was growing a tatty little beard which on a younger man might have given him a bohemian edge but now made him look frankly even more disreputable.

I bought him a Cognac and we went out back for a ciggy. I noticed his hand was shaking when he lit up. I made small talk and let the brandy settle into his system. I ordered another round and we returned to the table. I knew he'd start to talk sooner or later. It would be money or women.

"All right Jules. Out with it - what's going on?"

He sat quietly for a minute, collecting his thoughts, and then looked forlornly at me.

"You're not going to fucking believe what's happened," he said.

"Try me," I said and sat back.

So, in between sips of coffee and Cognac, and with nervous glances towards the door at the front of the bar, he began to tell me his story.

"You remember my new book launch?" he asked.

"*New* book? I thought it was all your old poems rehashed?" I said. With the recent upswing of popular interest in poetry Jules had been 're-discovered'. The poet manqué had been granted a final fling at literary stardom thanks to an enterprising but ridiculously optimistic Parisian publishing house.

"Yes, yes, it was, that doesn't matter, but when we had the big launch party I met this girl."

"Of course, Jules, you met a girl, *quelle surprise mon amis*".

"Don't be facetious George," he retorted. "This is damned serious."

I couldn't help the wry smile that appeared on my face. You would have felt the same in my shoes. Jules had indulged in a string of love affairs, trysts and encounters and none of them had ended in any kind of permanent relationship so far as I could tell. After the romantic dramas were over, I was used to keeping him company while he cried into his Merlot for a few days, then, usually within an indecently short interval, he would re-emerge apparently devoid of guilt or yearning, fresh and ready to fall for the next pretty little muse that crossed his path.

He took another glug of brandy and leaned

conspiratorially towards me, speaking sotto voce, "Her name was Valentina, Russian, an absolute beauty George, and she was at the launch party. She just came up to me and asked me questions about some of my early stuff, you remember, the White Room, Midnight Mass, Risk and Reward. I couldn't believe it - she knew them all. She was quoting lines from poems I couldn't remember myself! And she asked these perceptive questions, she wasn't just a typical Lit student. Gorgeous hazel eyes, like limpid pools you could just dive into."

He paused, then with a terribly melodramatic sigh he said, "Oh fuck, fuck, fuck, what have I done?"

I was largely unmoved. So far, so typical Jules I thought. The latest in a long line of liaisons which generally morphed rapidly from mutual infatuation to disillusionment as the object of his affections began to peel away the layers of affectation to reveal the real Jules. Who was the real Jules anyway?

I've known Jules since he and I were at the same minor public school in Hampshire. Yes, he was that irritating boy that managed to do remarkably well in exams with apparently minimal levels of preparation. And yes, the time he saved on swotting was devoted to chasing local village girls or ghost writing love letters for spotty fourth formers with crushes on sixth form girls (or boys). But a poet? A poet in

Paris? Let's get real, as they say these days. After a few University meet-ups it was ten years before any of us got wind of him. We had assumed he would be blagging it in some over-paid City trader job or scamming his way into the arms of a billionaire's daughter. Neither of those outcomes would have surprised us in the slightest. But to learn that he had taken up residence in Paris and somehow become the clarion of a kind of edgy new genre of poetry and with two acclaimed volumes to his name, well, you can imagine - what a con! Occasionally he'd even appear on late night arts review shows on the BBC, in his black polo neck, trying to look like bloody Jean-Paul Sartre! That must have been the Eighties – a time of fervent capitalist emancipation when his contrarian anti-establishment scribbles, his retro 'poetry of the people' found a half-decent following in socialist enclaves from Nottingham to Notting Hill.

Anyway, he blathered on with his story, "I loved her George I really did," he mewed. 'God this is going to be excruciating', I thought.

Jules took a deep breath and plunged on. "We met again at the Musée D'Orsay. We hardly saw the paintings because we talked so much about art, poetry, music. Cézanne, Mandelstam, Moussorski – she was incredibly knowledgeable. She said she had always loved my work – even as a girl she had somehow got hold of a copy of The White Room and memorised every poem. Imagine that! I know what you are thinking. Young enough to be my daughter etcetera etecetera, but not really, I mean she was twenty-eight years old George, that's hardly jailbait."

"After a couple of weeks, I admit I was head over heels, like nothing I've felt before. She was in Paris to study the language – staying with friends of her parents who wouldn't approve of her meeting me. We met every day usually at a Museum or gallery and then back to my place. I can't begin to tell you George, her skin was like ivory silk, unblemished. And when we made love she was passionate and demanding. Her voice, her Russian accent, it was all so damned sexy - I couldn't believe my luck."

I feared he was about to go into some sordid intimate details about his bedroom antics but to his credit he paused and then said, "Like an idiot I spoiled it all."

"What happened?" I asked. (I confess, I was mildly intrigued.)

"There were times she couldn't meet me. Lunches, dinners. I wanted to take her out for the evening, to a restaurant, to a club, to show her off a bit, but she wasn't available; she said she had to be home or go out with her parents' friends. To begin with I convinced myself it didn't matter but then, typical bloody me, I became jealous and suspicious. Why did we always meet at a museum in the morning or afternoon? Was she seeing someone else? Where did she live? So, one day I followed her."

"Christ Jules, I am seriously beginning to wonder if you have lost your marbles, if you have any left that is" I said.

"In a way, you're right, I have. You haven't heard the half of it yet. I followed her as carefully as I could. I lost her on the Métro the first time but on the second occasion, after she left me at the Palais Royal, she continued on foot. I trailed her to the Avenue Montaigne. And you know where she went? Into that fucking big palace hotel, the Plaza Athenée! Now that place is glitzy ritzy and a thousand euros a night plus, so what the hell is a poor little Russian language student doing there? I gave it ten minutes then I went to reception and said I had a meeting with a guest, Valentina Leonov. My heart was pounding, and I was sweating. Sure enough, they started dialling through to a room."

"For Christ's sake," I said, "what was she doing there? What did you do?"

"Just hold your horses," said Jules, and continued, "Well I panicked. I gave a false name and obviously I scarpered quick as I could. I was shocked – what the hell was she playing at!? We were due to meet again the next day and of course my mind went into complete jelly meltdown trying to figure it out. Like a complete fool I decided I had to know the truth, so I asked her outright. She didn't look embarrassed or anything, but she became angry and upset. She accused me of mistrusting her, she who had 'risked' everything to be with me. She said she had told me she could not meet at her place and why had I messed everything up, why did I have to question it? I was astonished George, I said I loved her and I just didn't understand why we couldn't meet like normal people and it was bugging me until I just had to see where she lived with my own eyes. She became very serious and solemn. She said her parents' friends were very wealthy but very private and security conscious, so she was staying as their guest in the hotel. She said I had spoiled things for her. I was never to come to the hotel again."

"I felt terrible, mortified," he continued. "I was her inspiration and I had soiled the whole beautiful experience."

"That's not how it seems from where I'm sitting" I said. "Did you believe her story about why she was at the hotel?"

"Yes, at first" Jules replied, "because I couldn't bring myself to consider any other explanation. But then things got the better of me. I tried to contact her, texts and calls – no response. I couldn't believe she wouldn't see me again. I had to see her. Finally, I heard from her and we met again - only this time, no museum, no café, no wine - she insisted we meet in the Luxembourg Gardens."

"I don't understand" I said, "What was her problem?"

"I didn't either" he said, "But I soon found out. She said

it had been a mistake, her seeing me, she was missing her important lessons and her parents' friends had found out and it would end badly. She said she loved me, it had been beautiful, and gave me some of her poems to read, but then suddenly she was standing up and saying goodbye. I couldn't believe it. She made me promise not to come looking for her – she said if I did it might end badly, there might be trouble. She said I wasn't to call her or text her."

I signalled to the barman for another round.

"Oh well, mon amis, you probably had the best of it – there's always another adventure around the corner *n'est cepas*?" I said.

"George, listen, it doesn't end there. If only it had! You see, when we met the previous time I checked her handbag when she went off to the loo. And I found her hotel key with the room number."

"Good grief! You didn't go back did you?" I exclaimed.

"I did. I went back to the hotel. I went to the room and knocked on the door. Big mistake. I expected her to open the door to a cute little hotel room. Ha! You should have seen it - a bloody great suite, living rooms, bedroom, all the shiniest decor and plush fittings you can imagine. But guess what? A swarthy muscular guy opened the door. Mean-looking as hell. I could see Valentina and another bloke in the background. The guy at the door starting shouting at me in

Russian and then looked back over his shoulder at the other two. Like an idiot I called out to Valentina, called out her name. Both blokes froze and immediately started speaking fast Russian to her. But I had come prepared. As things were evidently getting heated I reached into my bag and handed the thug at the door a book of my poems and I shouted out to Valentina, 'Here is the signed copy that you wanted. Au revoir!' and scuttled off, fully expecting to feel a heavy hand on my shoulder before I made it to the lift."

"Bloody hell Jules, you are probably lucky to be in one piece! Who the hell were those people and what was she doing with them?" I said.

"There's more. It gets worse." he said gloomily. We stepped outside for air and a smoke. The barman brought our drinks out to us and Jules carried on, "So obviously after that I didn't go back to the hotel and I lay in bed at night unable to sleep, just imagining all the possible scenarios. Were those her parents' friends? Seemed very unlikely! The guy at the door looked like some kind of henchman. A suite at that place can cost an absolute fortune – could they be Russian businessmen, or worse the mafia or something like that? I was in despair until a few days later I received a postcard from Valentina, here, look."

He took a dog-eared card out of his jacket pocket. I read the hastily written script on the back. It said:

*'Jules, I loved you, but it is over. I am so sorry I lied to you. I come to Paris to study French and get a job but then I met these people and now I am with them. They look after me, but they are not nice people, not like you. You deserve a better girl than me. I hope you like my poetry. I will always love yours – don't ever stop writing. Do not contact me again. I send a card because they check my phone messages. I think they suspect something. It was beautiful. Valentina x'*

"Wow. If I wasn't such an old cynic I'd have a tear in my eye. That was a close shave old boy!" I said.

But Jules wasn't finished.

"I thought it was really over, the whole thing. It had been such a roller-coaster and my emotions were all over the place. I stayed at home, watched TV, drank and slept. Then about ten days ago - I'll never forget the date, it was Thursday the twelfth. I was on my bed reading when there was a knock on the door. Normally people buzz up from the street but sometimes a neighbour lets people in. Stupidly I opened the door a fraction and it was immediately pushed in my face and I was knocked backwards by these two blokes. I recognised one of them from the hotel room. Have you ever been in a fight or been brave in a situation like that George? Me neither. I mean look at me, I'm fifty-two and I drink and smoke and I don't exercise. Plus, I'm basically a physical coward, so you can start to imagine my thoughts at that moment. These guys were like something out of a gangster movie. Close shaven heads, black jeans, leather jackets. I said something stupid like, 'Can I help you?' The taller guy pinned me to the wall of my living room and shoved my signed book of poems in my face right against my nose. Jesus, I was scared stiff. He said something like, 'You fucking with Valentina you fucking trash you die' – don't quote me on that – it came with a heavy hit of alcohol breath and strong Russian accent. 'No no, not at all, no fucking', I said 'just poetry, she student I am teacher - no fucking!' At this point the other guy opened the door onto my balcony – at that moment I swear George, I thought my life was over."

Jules was shaking so I put my hand on his shoulder and said, "It's OK, you're OK old man. What the hell happened next?"

"They lifted me up like a bag of sugar and took me out onto the balcony. They held me with my head and arms hanging out over the metal railing, so I was in mid-air waving my hands desperately trying to catch hold of something solid while the street below loomed up at me. I'm embarrassed to say I shat myself. I was out of this world with fright - the worst feeling of my life."

"Fuck" I said. I couldn't think of another word.

Jules spluttered out the rest of his story. "They waved me around like that for what seemed like an eternity and the big guy shouted 'Next time you fuck with Valentina we fuck with you – yes? Next time we say bye bye, ok? Understand my friend?' Then it was over, they yanked me in and dropped me in a heap on the floor and they just sauntered out of my place like they had popped in to read the fucking meter."

"Bloody hell old man" I said, and then after a few moments, "Jules, you are coming back to mine right now"

I got him home to mine and for the next week or so I took care of him like a father with his errant son. He was a wounded man. I'd never seen him like this, with no reserves, running on empty, shaking, crying, drinking. Gradually he began to come around. I got him shaven and looking presentable again, cooked him some healthy meals and monitored his alcohol consumption. Eventually we ventured out and had a few lightweight bevvies, took in a couple of shows. He looked nervously over his shoulder a lot, but he got through it. After ten days I went back with him to his bolt-hole on the Rue Saint-Martin, near the Marais. It's typically Jules, bohemian, scruffy, a stiff walk up the stairs to the top floor but it's full of character and of course there's the now infamous balcony. I confess I envy him his pad, the view over the roof-tops. Anyway, we tidied up a bit, and he seemed OK.

So, I left him, a chastened, humbled man; ashamed,

embarrassed, humiliated. Unlike all the previous times it seemed like after this experience the scars would be deep and permanent and for once he wouldn't bounce back or reinvent himself. I called from time to time and he said he was 'doing OK - sleeping better', though he told me in earnest detail how he had installed triple deadlocks and security cameras.

Well, the truth is my Samaritan streak only goes so far and after a while I suppose I just got on with my life and if I thought about Jules at all I assumed he was licking his wounds and perhaps even contemplating a change of direction. Maybe he'd leave Paris, give up the literary scene and try something new?

Then, about eighteen months later I read this review in L'Express:

*Jules Moncrieff's latest volume is a revelation. Where his previous work The Air Factory scathingly mocked the efforts of the western powers to introduce effective measures to minimise environmental impact, this new series of poems, The Russian Doll, thirty-two in all, is on a much more intimate level, a tour de force of relationship angst and existential rage. Alive with raw emotion and vivid imagery, many are set in Moncrieff's beloved Paris, but this time the romantic appeal of the city is searingly interlaced with dark menace. In "Vertical View" the sense of alienation, fear and loneliness is tangible, and the traffic noise and pollution become visceral reminders of a new singular sense of identity, whereas in the eponymous "Russian Doll", the poet questions whether we can really know ourselves or the true soul of others when there is always the prospect of hidden layers being revealed. This volume is a splendid, unexpected gift from the master of surprises.*

# The Concierge

## October 2000

At around half past three every weekday afternoon Jeanne's habitual indulgence was to switch on the radio, (she preferred the old chansons and had an especially soft spot for Jacques Brel), settle down into her comfy armchair, take the weight of her tired feet and smoke a leisurely cigarette or three. The entrance steps were scrubbed and the brass polished, the tiled floors in the hall washed, the mail sorted. As was her custom, she'd been out early to the local shops to buy fresh fish or chicken and vegetables for her dinner, had a pleasant chat with Céline in the boulangerie and a quick coffee with her pal Audré. Now she could relax, and the rest of the day was hers to enjoy.

Except that wasn't to be the case on this particular Wednesday in early May. Over half way through her first Gitanes, the front door bell went.

"*Mais qu'est-ce qui se passe maintenant,*" she grumbled

to herself. Probably another damned delivery for an absent resident. Sometimes her little apartment resembled a parcel sorting office. She shuffled over to the intercom in her day slippers. "Oui?" Twenty years as a concierge had given her the habit of conveying both authority and impatience in just one word.

Conor stood on the stone steps outside the imposing door, his ear pressed to the ancient intercom, when the bark came through. "*Ah oui bonjour Madame, je m'appelle Conor Seagate et je cherche . . .*," he rattled on nervously with his best French, normally fluent, but suddenly feeling unpractised and awkward coming from his lips. "I am looking for someone, a girl, called Julie, she used to live here, and I did too, it was ten years ago . . . is there any possibility . . . do you think you could help me?"

"There's no Julie here," replied Jeanne, eyeing with some irritation the dying embers of her cigarette and wondering if that was an American or British accent. It was hard to tell. Not French anyway and certainly an annoying interruption to her afternoon break. She hung up and went back to her chair, lit another cigarette and opened the paper to see what films might be worth catching at the weekend. The buzzer went again.

"*Oh, mon dieu!*" she exclaimed, leaning forward with the paper on her knee, pausing to see if they would give up or ring again.

Outside the building Conor had stood for several minutes taking in the surroundings. Although ten years had passed, the Rue Samarande hadn't really changed. A few swankier shops on the corner near the boulevard maybe, and a lick of grey paint on the front door of number 19, where he stood now, but on the whole, it still conveyed the same appealing grandeur of the elegant Haussmann facades. He couldn't give up now. He hadn't flown ten hours across the Atlantic to just walk away. Or was this curt rejection to be his rather pathetic destiny? Was this trip all a *grande folie*, to be demolished in a few terse words by a recalcitrant housekeeper? He rang the concierge's bell a third time. This time, after quite a long delay, the voice was even more intimidating.

"*Oui, mais qui est la*?!"

"*Oui Madame, je m'excuse, mais . . .*" and he tried again using as much charm and persuasion as he could muster. "Madame, forgive me but I am on a quest to find a missing person and she lived here in Apartment 5 in this house in 1990, and do you mind if I ask you if you were the concierge at that time? Because if you were or if you have any information – really, anything at all - I would be most grateful to you. It is terribly important because I must find her. Her name was Julie," he trailed off.

Jeanne had these random callers from time to time, always claiming that they were in search of someone or something terribly important. What strange lives people led! But number 19 was a big house, once a private mansion, now the home of (mostly) respectable Parisians and a few wealthy foreigners who owned vacation apartments. These days Jeanne prided herself on knowing her residents and even knowing some of their business, but ten years before it had been a different story - a lot of the apartments were rented out in those days and there were endless comings and goings of tenants and students – what a nightmare it used to be. Now the street had gone up in the world and with that transformation had come a matching change in Jeanne.

There was a time when she had felt to be unappreciated, the low-caste hired help, down on her luck, having to endure the bitter consequences of her misfortune and her poor decisions in life. She took consolation in reading or going to the movies, imagining herself as a character from a novel by Victor Hugo or in a moody film by Truffaut or Godard, weaving into her identity some of their existential fatalism and even adopting certain dramatic behaviours and gestures. But in the last decade she had also reclaimed a little pride, not so much in her apartment which she knew to be shabby, but deeper within herself, by letting go of the past and at the same time appreciating the greater degree of authority she enjoyed as concierge now that the building and its residents had gone up in the world. She was not just the key-holder and cleaner any longer, she had some status. Some of the residents felt she behaved more like the chatelaine than the concierge and they had become rather timid in their requests, which rather pleased Jeanne, who could exhibit haughty disdain on cue.

Conor craned his neck towards the intercom; he could hear that she hadn't put the receiver down because there was still some hissing and crackling, and then the voice spoke again. "I'm sorry Monsieur, I cannot help you." The hissing stopped, and the connection went dead.

Jeanne was intent on returning to her chair and her paper, but something made her pause en route and she found herself momentarily lost in thought. Instead, she walked into her kitchen and rested her hands on the counter, looking out through her lace blinds at the shapes of the houses opposite. She had an instinct for trouble – it served her well as a concierge – but now a different instinct was directing her thoughts back in time. By kneeling on her kitchen stool, she could get an angle from her window to just see the street in front of the house. A man was standing there looking at the building, carrying something over his shoulder. He was tall, with fair hair, in his thirties she imagined, a good-looking boy - American or Scandinavian perhaps.

As she watched him standing outside the front door some fragments of memory began to coalesce into a vague idea in her mind, and she got down from the stool and walked slowly across the apartment into her bedroom, opened the door to her cupboard and switched on the light. As the bare bulb illuminated the dusty shelves and she reached up to retrieve a papier maché box the idea started to become a more defined thought - there was just the flicker of a possible connection. She leafed through the contents of the box of memorabilia: black and white photos of Serge and their friends from the fifties, bleached Polaroids and faded prints of early family life in the sixties and later. That pitiful letter from the German officer to his family – the builders had discovered it under the boards when the apartments were converted. She put it aside along with the letters and cards from her son and from various old friends until she found it - the postcard with the Matisse painting. And on the reverse in a large flowing script in green ink.

*If Conor Seagate should ever come to look for me, please give him this.*

*Conor, I can't believe you are reading this. You're crazy! (Me too). I had to leave Paris for work. Come and find me?*

An address in Hong Kong, then a signature:

## Julie

It must have been three years, maybe four years or more when she had called at number 19 to talk briefly to Jeanne. A vivacious young woman, with warm dark eyes and long fair hair, quite charming and insistent that Jeanne would keep the card safe. It was silly she said, but you never knew, just in case.

Conor remained standing outside the house for some minutes. He didn't know what to do next. It had been foolish to place too much hope on this one possibility. Ten years was such a long time. But ten years ago, Conor and Julie had been here, in Flat 5 at the top of this house, looking out over the grey slate rooftops. Here was where she rented a place with her student friends from the Sorbonne and here was where he visited her, where they were always happy to return, walking arm in arm from evenings at clubs and concerts. Here was where they had talked and laughed and fallen in love, suddenly and inevitably. Here they made love on her single bed and talked into the early hours, sometimes watching the dawn light come softly over the covers, just lying and watching each other. Here is where they had imagined who and where they would be ten years on at the turn of the millennium, the unthinkable year 2000. And one day, when she knew he was soon going to have to return to the States, she had said: 'Let's make a vow, wherever our lives take us, let's meet up in ten years and if we are free, let's be together again forever.' And she had given him her precious Thai amulet and said it would bring him luck.

Julie, the free-spirit, the idealist, the dreamer, had said those special words. And so, when they eventually parted, he treasured her words and nurtured them, kept them close to his heart. He kept the amulet as a souvenir, so he should never forget her. It was his lucky talisman to ward off the dreadful possibility that life might never again be so wonderful and joyful as his time with Julie in Paris, in 1990.

And now here he was, a romantic fool, ten years later, a grown man of thirty-three, with a childish wish that the amulet might still have some residual power or some meaning because . . . because in truth his life had indeed not been so wonderful ever again. And because he was prone to philosophising and wondering, 'do we make up our lives like the authors of our own stories and can we really choose what happens or is someone else rolling the dice?'

Inside her apartment, Jeanne stood quietly in her cupboard holding the card. The connection was clear now. He had said his name was Conor - she pictured him standing at that very moment outside the house, perhaps wondering which turn his life would take. Or would he have walked away, was it already too late? And if it was too late, well, she thought 'C'est la vie, n'est-ce pas?' She stared at the tattered box which contained not only the postcard from Julie but also all the memories of the twists and turns of her own life, each one a bitter-sweet offering to the Gods of love and loss, a paean to the vicissitudes of fate.

This simple box held the memories of pain and regret but also of love and warmth, and these mixed emotions now welled up uncomfortably in her chest. Carefully and deliberately Jeanne shut the lid of the box, placed it back on the shelf, switched off the light and closed the cupboard.

She opened the door of her apartment and stepped quietly into the hall. As she walked towards the front door of the house she spoke to herself in her mind. 'Ten seconds. If he is still there I will invite him in, if he has gone then he has gone. It's not for me to decide.'

With a shrug of resignation Conor slung his bag over his shoulder and was turning to walk away when he heard the click of the door latch behind him. He looked back to see an elderly woman standing half in and half out of the doorway of number 19. She was probably in her seventies, a little world-worn, but with quite striking features, slim, with wavy hair, probably dyed, wearing a faded floral housecoat and a pair of Chinese embroidered slippers on her small feet. And suddenly he remembered her from all the times he visited Julie here in this house. She was formidable then and looked even more so now.

"Well, I suppose you had better come in then," said Jeanne, with an air of impatience.

Back inside the apartment Jeanne disappeared into her kitchen to make coffee, leaving Conor standing in the centre of the cluttered salon, with his backpack at his feet, a small dog sniffing him as he took in his surroundings. It was like a vintage furniture store he decided, a kind of time-warp. Over the fireplace was a curved thirties mirror with weathered glass. The armchairs were covered in faded, frayed fabrics and throws. The sofa, like a relic from a theatre set, was part-buried in old film magazines and what looked like knitting patterns and holiday brochures. There wasn't much natural light in the room and it was lit by an assortment of standard lamps and reading lights. There was a rather sickly aroma of perfume, nicotine and dog.

But still he was here, and his heart was racing. She had let him in. Would she have any idea how to find Julie? What were the chances? How much should he tell her?

Jeanne returned with the coffee and asked him to sit down, gesturing towards a decrepit chair that looked like it might abandon its life at any moment.

She sat opposite him, paused to light a cigarette and then began to speak in a quiet but confident tone. "Now listen. My name is Jeanne Colbert. I remember Julie, but I don't remember you. You had better tell me who you are and why you are looking for her."

Conor told her how he and Julie had met at a party and quickly become friends, how she had lived here during her final year at University and he had been on a short intensive language course and how he had stayed on as long as he possibly could, a couple of months, before he had to return to the States. They had written of course but then, during the summer of the same year, he stopped receiving replies to his letters. He assumed she had moved out of the house or more likely met someone else. Though it was painful to consider that possibility, eventually the intensity of his feelings faded a little and he resigned himself to never seeing her again. He told Jeanne how in the ten years since then he had become an accomplished language teacher and travelled the world on assignments, yet though he had met other women and had relationships there had never been the passion and deep connection he had felt for Julie. So instead of the memory fading he found that he wanted to try and remember more and more of the details of their brief affair and each time he returned to Paris in later years he found he was compelled to revisit the left bank streets and cafes they had frequented. And on each visit, he would unearth another few precious shards and nuggets of memory, which he would nurture and embellish in his day-dreams. But still he never heard from Julie.

Conor was surprised to find himself pouring out more of his soul than he expected to this woman who was really a complete stranger. She sat and listened to him, nodding occasionally with a kind of wry smile on her face, sipping her coffee, studying him, smoking her cigarettes. A little drama had arrived on her doorstep and she was going to enjoy it.

"So that is my story. I can't tell you anymore," he said at last.

There was a silence between them and they both digested the moment, until Conor took a long breath and said, "So, Madame Colbert, can you please put me out of my misery, do you actually know where I can find Julie?"

Jeanne took another puff from her cigarette and blew the smoke out of the side of her mouth, before replying.

"Maybe, it depends."

"Depends on what?"

"It depends on me and it depends on you."

"I don't understand."

Jeanne leaned forward towards him, her arm tilted to one side and her cigarette hand pointing theatrically outwards. She pictured herself in a scene from an old movie. With an elaborate shrug of her shoulders she said, "Young man, what purpose is to be served in digging up the past? Do you think that Julie will be waiting for you with her arms open, just because you turn up out of the blue declaring your love? Do you imagine that this foolish notion of meeting ten years later is really something meaningful? We all say these things my dear, we are all drawn to the fairy story, we all want to meet the one, the one who will love us unconditionally. So, we believe in the story – but that is all it is, it's just a story you have told yourself."

Conor was taken aback. 'Why do I have to listen to her opinion?' he thought to himself.

"Well maybe, but it's my story not yours so I don't see what you believe has to do with anything."

"Well then you are free to go mon cher," Jeanne retorted, with a sardonic smile that left Conor nonplussed.

He couldn't figure out this old woman, Jeanne. She was disarming. In all the visits he'd made to the apartment during his time with Julie he had only seen her, this Jeanne Colbert, as the grouchy concierge giving him disapproving looks as she peered from her doorway into the hall to see who was coming and going. What right did she have to lecture him on his life? She was just the concierge, a glorified housekeeper. Yet he stayed put, sitting awkwardly in her strange apartment, because he felt he had no choice. She seemed to have some knowledge, but she was hiding it from him, or playing a game of cat and mouse.

He tried again asking a direct question about Julie, but Jeanne evaded the question and again she leaned forward and fixed him with a glare, and this time he detected an undercurrent of resentment or anger in her voice.

"This Julie, supposing she is now living somewhere happily married, with some little children and a nice husband? Eh? But perhaps there is a place in her heart that has remained empty despite her nice cosy marriage, a little nagging strain in her soul? And then Romeo comes along out of the blue and tugs on her heartstrings and twists her fate? What happens then eh? What happens to you and her and to her children and her husband? Are there lives not changed forever?"

"But if that is the case then I would walk away and accept the situation!" protested Conor.

"Oh, you think so do you, you who have come five thousand kilometres on your crusade from America to find the true love of your life! You with the lonely soul, you would be like a hungry dog looking for a scrap of love, any morsel, like my little Gaston here," gesturing to the dog, "he will eat any morsel of food and take any scrap of love. Let me tell you something, young Sir Galahad, you on your romantic quest – yes, I can see you are surprised by my language and you think maybe I am not so stupid for an old concierge! But just imagine . . . I have had all this time on my hands you see, time to think and time to read and to reflect. Years and years, you have no idea. Surely you have heard the expression 'you must not tempt fate'? Yes, I see you nod your head, of course you have heard it but let me tell you it means nothing, *rien du tout*, until you have lived it and paid the price. I was like you once, stars in my eyes, sunsets in my dreams, all my lovely future ahead of me."

Now Conor began to realise that he had no bargaining power in this strange encounter. He could make no more demands of this formidable lady. Either she would give him what he hoped for, if she actually knew anything, or she was just a crazy, lonely woman and he would lose an hour of his life listening to her and then he would move on. But until then she held the stage and was completely in control of this scene. His only faint hope was to listen to her and to see what would transpire. He could see she was animated now, as she stood up and lit another cigarette and walked back and forth across the living room, as if weighing up her thoughts and deciding what to say next. Eventually she stood still, with her hand resting on the mantelpiece, deep in thought. When was the last time she had told anyone? Was her life so inconsequential? Was she not entitled to tell her story once more if it might do some good and help this poor fool? She took another puff, blew the smoke slowly from her mouth and continued.

"Let me tell you a story. After the war France was like a different country - you would not recognise it. It took years for things to get back to normal, there was the destruction, all the missing relatives, the economy, we were wounded not just in our bodies but deep in our souls. Today everything is so bright and colourful so of course you don't realise, but in those days life was grey, and I was a young woman from the country and I craved bright lights and I came to Paris in the early fifties to get a job. I fell in with a fun crowd, we didn't have much money but still we met up at the cafes and we went to the *bals* and danced, and it was fun, it was enough."

She leaned towards the mirror, glanced in it, took another drag on her cigarette and said, "And then I met Serge."

She sighed at this point and sat down again, as if the mention of his name had drained the energy from her body. She sank right back into the chair, leaned to one side and rested the side of her head in her hand.

Conor sat motionless, unsure whether to say anything – he looked at Jeanne and she appeared to be in a reverie, staring without blinking at the flickering electric fire. Where was this story leading?

In her trance, she remembered sitting at a table on the terrace outside the Café Marne, sipping a champagne cocktail and smoking Russian gold foiled cigarettes. Her hair was auburn, coiffured into a fashionable demi-wave, and she wore a Dior summer suit. Her lipstick was carmine, and her shoes were chocolate, crocodile. She was waiting for

Serge. She pictured him, rolling up in his new cabriolet wearing a crisp white shirt and a dapper waistcoat – always a shiny new motor car for Serge – with his olive skin, dark eyebrows and swarthy good looks he was nothing like the pasty faced ill-nourished Parisians she had met. People said he was half Marseilles and half Moscow, he had the guile and gold-toothed charm of a port-side pirate and the charisma and presence of a prince from the Steppes.

After minutes of silence Jeanne lifted her head and looked again at Conor.

"It was after the war when I met him. Handsome, thrilling, fun to be with. For six months we were hand and glove, inseparable. I wanted the glamour and excitement of his life and he wanted me – I was very attractive in those days – of course it is hard to believe now – and with the money he showered on me and my friends, well, suddenly I was the elegant and chic girl about town. Restaurants, shows at the Moulin Rouge, there was racing at Le Mans, weekends at Deauville, nothing was too much. I never questioned where the money was coming from or whether it would last. We just lived in an endless present moment, the past was gloomy and painful and why think about the uncertain future when the present had everything you could want."

"What happened"? asked Conor.

Jeanne paused, then looked straight at Conor. "Ah so

innocent you are! What do you think happened? One day I was waiting as usual after work, all dolled up and ready to go out and, he just didn't turn up. Nothing, no message, silence. The days went by like a terrible bad dream and I spoke with friends and tried to piece things together. Some business deal gone wrong – away on an emergency – different versions of events. After a while the shock subsided a little and I realised that I knew little of Serge's daily life, I was so naive. Then a phone call, apologising, and then a letter, promising me he would be back, he had to go to America on urgent business. I was ecstatic with relief, but it was so confusing. Then, inevitably, nothing. He just disappeared. I have to tell you . . . it simply broke my heart."

"I'm so sorry" said Conor. He was genuinely moved by her story, but he couldn't wait to get back to his life, to his story, so a few moments later he gathered himself together and said, "But Madame, what has this to do with me and Julie?"

"Because, dear young man, it is only when you get to my age that you can look down from the top of the mountain and you can see the paths and the valleys where you have been – and – also with some regret you may also see the paths you did not take. And here we are today – look at us - yes, we are an odd couple, aren't we?" – she smiled, quite a sweet, endearing smile – "but we are here in this moment together and you are seeking to take a turn in your life. Quite a dramatic and potentially unexpected turn is it not? And one that may have consequences, not necessarily good, for you and for the girl you seek. Can you begin to see what you are doing? How can you? You are nowhere near the top of the mountain! In fact, you are really wandering blindly in the forest letting your feelings take you in unexpected directions."

"Yes, I suppose that's true," replied Conor and as he spoke he reached into his shirt and touched the amulet. "But my feelings are profound and real, and I feel that if I don't try to find her and at least speak to her then I will regret it all my life."

Jeanne stood up again and paced across the room. Well, she thought, I have started this strange little scene so now I am going to finish it.

"I know I know," she replied, "you feel it in your heart and I once had feelings that were that strong and so young man I understand what has brought you here today, but should we allow feelings alone to determine the course of our lives?" She went on. "You see, sixteen years after Serge disappeared and left me, left me like a washed-up pretend princess, he came into my life again. It was in '68, the year of the student riots. There was a kind of craziness in the air. By then I was married with a child, my husband was a good man, a steady, sound man, with a good corporate job, and we had a house in Vincennes. I worked in administration - just an ordinary pen-pushing, part-time job but one day in a magazine I saw an advertisement. It was an invitation to some kind of business opportunity, to attend a seminar, something to do with the military. To be honest I didn't fully understand it, but that is beside the point. You see, on the advertisement there was a photo of the speaker and it was Serge. There was no doubt about it. Only this time he was called Sergei not Serge, but I knew it was him."

Conor was intrigued now, temporarily forgetting where he was and the purpose of his mission.

"What did you do?"

"What do you think? What could I do, it was destiny. I went along to see for myself if it was really him."

"You're kidding?" said Conor, "And what happened?"

"What happened? Yes, that is what we all want to know, but we should ask more what WILL happen, because afterwards it is too late to figure it all out and place it in a tidy box." Jeanne paused. Conor thought he saw her eyes shining with emotion now as she spoke. "What happened was I went to the lecture and indeed it was Serge, or Sergei as he called himself, still with the same tremendous good looks and charm but now half-French half-American sounding, trying to drum up business, get investments I suppose for his latest scheme. And then, now listen to me carefully, then you must understand, I made a terrible mistake. Instead of walking out of the room, I waited until the end and I went to speak to Serge and – well – do I need to tell you what happened after that? Although he had changed, we both had of course after sixteen years, but still there was that magnetism, that feeling, and we could not pretend it wasn't there. So, like a foolish girl, I began an affair with him."

"It was passionate and exciting, but also furtive and deceitful and I quickly began to feel ashamed of myself. But still I carried on, we carried on for several months, until, my God, it was so awful, until my husband found out. Someone at my work ratted on me and we were confronted – there were no excuses, no chance to even lie or bluff my way out. Just bare-faced deception and cheating. And, it is worse, because I loved him so much I also invested a great sum of money, taken from our family savings, and I trusted it in Serge's scheme. But it was not a serious scheme, more of a crooked deception as it turned out, because the money was never returned or recovered – you see in the end he was just a charmer, a con artist. And because of that utterly stupid selfish decision I have paid a terribly high price. My husband was incensed and ashamed and refused to take me back. In the end he gave me some money and an allowance for our boy and I started a new life on my own."

Jeanne paused, finishing her monologue. "Of course, this happened a very long time ago but what matters is that it is the main story of my life, of how I eventually answered an advertisement to become the concierge here at number nineteen, and so you saw me ten years ago and so you see me now. Et voila."

Conor was speechless at first as he digested her account. As she talked he began to see that she was warning him. It was obvious, yet still in his naivety and his arrogance he figured it was his life and why should her story, however tragic, have any bearing on what he chose to do? And perhaps his narrative would have a happier ending than hers?

At last he spoke, with care, trying not to upset her further, "Jeanne, I understand what you are saying, and I am truly sorry that you lost your husband and things did not turn out the way you hoped, but must this be my destiny too? I mean there are a hundred different possible endings aren't there? And mine could be different? And besides, I desperately need to know if this means you know where Julie is or how I can contact her?"

But now Jeanne had become exhausted. She had scarcely told her story more than half a dozen times in thirty years and each time it took a profound emotional toll.

She knew that this moment in Conor's life might be deeply significant with all kinds of unpredictable consequences and yet he wanted to rush in with all the reckless energy of youth. She felt the heavy burden of responsibility upon her – she could deny him what he craved and so perhaps determine the course of his life and protect the lives of others. She could give him Julie's card and then another set of events would be entrained. Her life since the last meeting with Serge had proved to be a hard road to travel and she knew she had been embittered by the experience. Visitors saw her as the bossy old concierge – could they just once see her as she was all those years ago, in her finery, laughing with friends at the bar, Serge pouring champagne, his warm hand on her back. She had become more closed and more cautious, measuring every little turn for what it was worth, what each outcome would be. More fearful, more cynical, taking it out on visitors who asked damned fool questions or muddied her pristine floors or complained about the electricity problems which had never been her responsibility. Had she become like a shrew in her old age? Was there still any lightness in her soul? And had she not once been full of romantic dreams and desires and although they had led to folly, but had they not also contained precious days and moments which were still revered? Shouldn't this young man be entitled to follow the strange course of his life and not have her memories sabotage his dreams?

Jeanne felt again the stirrings of a mysterious delight in

this role, as she saw herself playing a brief but pivotal part in someone else's life once more. She rose from her chair and went to the cupboard. She opened again the memento box and there sitting alongside all her cherished memories was a simple postcard which was perhaps, on reflection, a greater treasure than all the others, because it could unlock a future yet untold, the story of a life whose narrative was perhaps just beginning, even as hers was closing.

She walked slowly back into the salon. Conor was standing up now, knowing that they had reached a turning point, but as to what kind he remained unsure. Until Jeanne spoke again, this time in a quieter, calmer voice. "Just a few years ago, your Julie came here to this house and she spoke to me with great purpose and intensity. It was a brief meeting, but it impressed me greatly. And she gave me this card to give to you should you ever re-visit. You will be very pleased to know that it contains an address."

Conor rocked back a little on his feet with sheer astonishment. He stood looking at Jeanne with his eyes widening. "All this time, you have had this card and you have known!?"

Jeanne held the card in both her hands and before handing it to Conor she looked carefully into his eyes and said, "I am sorry that I did not tell you immediately. I am just a foolish old woman and I have taken up your afternoon with my memories. Please be careful what you wish for and which turns you choose to take in your life. Every turn has a hidden consequence. It is seldom gifted to us to see what will happen. I wish I had taken more care along the way and that is my message to you. But it's your journey now - you have my blessing in this." And she reached across with both hands and gave him Julie's card.

Conor read the card and looked at Jeanne, with tears beginning to form in his eyes. He could only manage a choked "Merci Madame, merci."

She showed him to the door and watched him lift his pack onto his back and wave shyly at her. "Bonne chance, bon courage!" she shouted to him.

Later that afternoon, after her nerves had calmed down a little, Jeanne telephoned her friend. "*Écoute*, listen Audré, don't ask why but we're going out, the champagne is on me. Six o'clock at Léon's – be smart!"

She rummaged in her wardrobe and found at the end of the rail the dress she had in mind, a flattering fawn and white cotton number which hadn't seen the light of day in years, but to her delight it still fitted. Then in a box at the back she found the heels she was looking for - brown crocodile that always pinched but still had a certain sexiness about them. Sitting in front of the mirror at her dressing table she added a double string of pearls, brushed her still wavy hair and fixed it with a tortoise-shell clip on the side. Never mind the grey starting to show through again - it would have to do. A spritz from an ageing bottle of Chanel No. 5 – it had been Serge's favourite ever since he heard that Monroe wore it. A fur stole across her shoulders, a quick brush of crimson lipstick and she was ready.

"It's as good as it's going to get," she said aloud, as she hitched Gaston to his lead. Together Jeanne and Gaston walked down Rue Samarande under the soft yellow light of the early evening street lamps. She lifted her chin, held the lead up high to make the little dog stop sniffing the pavement, and the two of them walked towards the corner with an unusual spring in their steps.

# The Blue Dress

## February 2006

Hank knew you can get an e-ticket and do all that stuff online, but he chose to use Sally down at the agency and they mailed him the old-fashioned printed tickets. Logan to Charles de Gaulle, February 13th, 2006.

Jeez that made him seventy-six and Lil seventy-three! What the heck, we're still going – no way are we going to miss it, even if the whole darned family kicks off. She's just forgetful that's all, comes to all of us. And he'd conceded a little hadn't he? I mean buying first class and a suite at the hotel – another three thousand bucks from the pension, just to be safe and make her comfortable. The tickets were sitting on top of the bow front chest in his study. He looked at them every day, touched them and checked the dates, like he was in front of a shrine. They'd been to Paris every couple of years for the last forty-nine, and now here they were once more, so everything was going to be ok.

He recalled the very first visit. It hadn't gone to plan, the proposal. Told the story at his expense so many goddamned times - everyone still laughs when they hear it. Planned it out in his boyish imagination; a walk along by the Seine in cosy winter coats, soft candle light in the restaurant, accordion music, some fancy chateau wine and he would make his move, the young gallant, on his knees with a diamond for the indescribably beautiful Lillian. But he'd got the restaurant names mixed up. They got lost, ate at a crappy tourist trap on the left bank while he sweated and fingered the ring box in his pocket. But on the way back, across the bridge, the moonlight on the river – he confessed his dumb plan and asked her outright if she'd consider marrying a fool who couldn't find his way round a big city. And they laughed and kissed and held the ring up to sparkle in the moonlight. He knew then he'd got the right girl. Stuck by her, like the old man said – commit to what you love son, see it through. And damn it he would. 'No-one knows her like me', Hank figured.

Lil was restless on the plane despite the pills. And he had to take her to the toilet and no matter what anyone tells you about the mile-high club no way can you get two people into those cubicles, so he had the door ajar and shouted instructions and hoped for the best. The intimacy was a new thing. Not the intimacy of sex, hell they'd known each other pretty well in that department, but now she had become forgetful about you know, going to the toilet and cleaning herself up and such. But it's just old age. At first the indignity, the embarrassment. But soon we got it figured, just like everything we ever did together, we found a way. Thinking back, she was a beauty but never prissy, never afraid to break a nail. Didn't we scrape and burn all the old paint off the doors, the shutters, the panelling and the porch until the house on the corner was peeled right back bare and ready for us to make it new? Nothing a lick of paint can't make fresh. Or a wash with soap and water. She was just a tad forgetful that's all.

Lillian wanted to close her eyes and lie down but the man wouldn't let her, said she had to stand up in line and show her passport. The man was Hank, of course he was. He said, "It's OK honey, we're back in Paris, show them your passport." The passport photo was her, it was Lillian, but looking unhappy. "I don't like this photo of me," she said. "It's not me." She slept in the cab from the airport. She followed Hank into the Hotel de Pantheon and seemed to recognise the lobby. "I love this place" she said, "We were here before, there was a piano in the bar and he played Brubeck. Do you remember?" She wandered down a hall, she was sure the bar and the piano man would be there, gentle hands sweeping across the white and black keys in the darkened room.

Installed in the fancy hotel suite, Hank walked her round the rooms – familiarisation was vital. "This is our home for a week hon; nice sofa, comfy chair, TV, here's the bathroom, a shower and a tub, two marble basins – his and hers! Here's the toilet, do you need to go? No, okay, so here's our bedroom, wow, some bed hey Lil? Look at this painting, who is this by?"

She knew it straightaway, "Gustav Klimt" she said quick as a flash, and then Hank said, "Look at these flowers Lil – tell me the names," and she said, "my flowers Hank, my lilies" and he kissed her and said, "I ordered them for you honey."

Lil walked around the rooms touching the fabrics and the furniture. Why had they changed the curtains? And where was the kitchen? She sat on the bed and started rocking and chewing a nail. Hank put his arm round her and said, "Time to sleep now Lil, everything will be fine tomorrow." He loved her like this, sleepily putting her head against his shoulder, like Elle used to do when she was five or six years old. Fine hair, silvery and wavy, twisted strands curling on the delicate skin of her temple, softly folded onto her cheeks. Like his, her skin was creasing and folding more and more with age, but he had long ago reconciled himself to the fact that they would never be young again. He loved her wrinkles which told the story of her life, all the laughter and some tears – it was good and honest.

Hank thought about Lil a lot. She was just getting more emotional, post-menopausal probably – she has her good days and bad like we all do, it's completely understandable. And her memory goes pretty wonky too but we all get like that. She's a fighter and she'll come out of this phase soon enough. But for now, he knew he had to take extra care, so the next day before they went out walking he took time to check she was okay to venture out and she knew that it might be busy on the streets. "So, what do you say to a stroll around Paris, hon, just like we used to? You think your nerves can handle it? Yes?"

Lil felt good. Paris, Paris. Her man on her arm. The beautiful storefronts, the quaint side streets, the brasseries and bars. Like a movie.

She said, "I came here with Jonny – we stayed at the Ritz and drank champagne cocktails."

Hank went along with it, "Uh huh, is that so Lil, and there was I thinking that it was me that took you to the Ritz, right?"

And Lil said, casually as you like, "Of course I know it was you. You played piano."

Hank never played piano, but she was spot on about the Ritz, that was their golden wedding. No idea who the heck

Jonny was but at least she remembered the rest. And she seemed happy, smiling and pointing out shops and buildings, holding close to him. She could be surprisingly affectionate these days, though sometimes cold and distant too. Truth was, deep down, it really troubled him.

In a quaint side-street in the Marais, Lil stopped in front of a vintage clothing store. She was staring at a blue dress on a mannequin in the window.

"That was my dress," she said.

"How do you mean hon?"

"My dress, when I got married."

"You got married in white sweetheart, I should know!"

"No, it was blue, it was this dress - why have they got my wedding dress?!"

"It's not your dress Lil, it's just a dress for sale."

"Why are they selling my wedding dress?" she asked again, insisting.

Hank said: "Let's go to that shop over there and check out those beautiful hats." Hank eased Lil away from the shop window, but she turned to look over her shoulder one more time. "Blue silk," she said.

She was over-excited, becoming anxious and tired. Hank hailed a cab and they went back to the hotel and stayed in, going to bed early.

The next day was Valentine's Day and Hank had his

plan. He was going to take Lil to a café on the quayside from where you could watch the Eiffel Tower light up.

The new day started well. He ordered them breakfast in their room. Eggs benedict, patisseries, fresh coffee. They sat by the window, holding hands. Still in their hotel dressing gowns they got comfy on the plush sofa and watched 'Breakfast at Tiffany's', Lil's favourite movie. It was just like old times thought Hank. Later they went and had tea in the hotel café and Lillian enjoyed watching the people come and go, commenting on the new fashions on display. Back in the room she said she wanted a bath, so Hank went to run it. He liked to get the water right for her. He looked at the expensive bottles of creams and lotions and poured in something called 'Mousse de Bain – Camelia'. Way too much! The bubbles were everywhere. "Hey Lil, check out the biggest bubble bath in the world!"

There was no answer. Not in the living room. She must be in the bedroom he thought. Not there. What the heck? "Lil, Lil!" he called. He looked around, the cupboard, the lobby? Nope. With rising panic, he went to the windows, but they showed no sign of being touched. He ran to the door and looked out both ways down the corridor – empty.

Hank grabbed his keys and his wallet and phone and ran along to the lift pressing the button again and again to hurry it up. His heart was beating fast, too fast. On the ground floor he burst out of the lift, pushing past people with suitcases, praying she would be there in the lobby, but still nothing. Then he remembered the piano man and she had thought it was down the hall, so he set off that way, sure that he would find her. But there was no bar, no piano, just some seminar rooms, all empty. "Jesus Christ!" he said.

Hank held his head in his hands. What the hell have I done? Where is she? What do I do now!? Okay fella, calm down, let's go tell the manager and get some help - there's gotta be a simple explanation.

And all the while he's explaining to the clerk at the desk, he's thinking, 'How will I forgive myself? How will I explain this to the kids?' And the clerk says "Well, Monsieur I expect your wife has just gone for a promenade or gone shopping". "No, you don't understand - you see she is a little forgetful. She wouldn't just do that". But then she would Hank, she would, she's already done it several times back home, he thought to himself.

"Please have a glass of water Monsieur and sit down for a minute, I will get the Manager". Hank sat on the edge of a huge leather sofa in the enormous lobby, feeling small, helpless and old. He felt palpitations coming on. He drank the cool water and took a heart pill. "Okay, think, think, where would she go?"

The Manager appeared and sat with him. He listened

carefully to what Hank had to say and then he said,

"Monsieur, if you are worried about your wife then we should report it now to the police as a missing person, and they will investigate."

'The police' Hank thought with rising alarm. A missing person? Yes, I guess that's what she is. It sounded ominous.

But then he looked across to the reception desk where a woman in a cream and blue dress was checking in and it dawned on him.

"I think I know where she might be!" he said.

"You know?" said the Manager, "so what is going on?"

"I have an idea where I can find her. There's a boutique a few blocks away – one of those places selling fancy second hand clothes - we walked past it yesterday and there was this blue dress. I am sure that's where she has gone!"

"Okay, said the manager, "Let me take you there by car – do you know the street?"

"I think I can show you" said Hank, and five minutes later they were in a Mercedes pulling away from the hotel entrance and Hank was looking at everyone he could see, catching glimpses of any elderly women in case they were Lil, even though they didn't look like her; trying to remember what she had on. White slacks? Pink or blue blouse? What if he was wrong? What if she was lost? Would she do something stupid?

The car waited for what seemed an eternity at traffic lights. He felt so bad, felt guilty, suddenly felt very alone. He decided to text his daughter. He was slow at texting, didn't use it much, didn't know what to say. "Hi Elle. I have lost Mum. But I think I know where she is. Going to find her. I am sorry. Pop" SEND.

To his amazement it was just a few seconds before his phone pinged and a message from Elle was there on the screen. "What do you mean you have LOST her!! I told you not to take her!! Have you called the Police? OMG, where did you see her last?"

Big mistake, in retrospect, sending that text. Must have been the stress and a guilty conscience.

They drove up and down streets that looked vaguely familiar, but there was no sign of the store. It had been different on foot. Then Hank remembered they had passed one of those Jewish bakeries before she saw the dress. The Manager did a U turn and headed down a side street, then suddenly across the road, thank God, there was the bakery and a few doors down the boutique and they double-parked right in front. The blue dress was not in the window. Good or bad sign? He didn't know. Maybe bad. They both hurried into the shop but there was no need to say anything more because, thank Christ, there was Lillian sitting on a chair with a glass of water in her hand. She looked up at Hank and smiled, just like nothing special had happened.

"Who is that man?" Lil said, looking at the hotel manager.

"It's alright hun, he's going to take us back to the hotel."

"Good," she said, "I want to go back to the hotel, with my dress."

Hank tried to explain to the boutique owner. He apologised. Truth was, he was at a loss as to what to think or do. The boutique owner told him Lil wanted to buy the blue dress, but when it came to pay she had no money or handbag, then she couldn't remember where she was staying and seemed confused, so the owner was about to call the emergency services.

Hank looked at Lil. Incredibly, she was smiling sweetly at him. "Don't forget my dress," she said.

The boutique owner seemed sympathetic. "Monsieur, your wife seems to think the dress is hers. She tried it on, but then she didn't want to take it off, so I told her I had to wrap it as a present and then she took it off. It is a very rare dress this Monsieur, very fine silk."

Hank knew there was only one option. He had to buy the dress. Turned out it was Chanel from the 1930's – at least that's what the lady said – and to be fair you could see the original label. *'Combien?'* Seven hundred and fifty euros! For a second-hand gown! But he knew there was no backing out.

The boutique owner had the dress all wrapped, the hotel manager had rather heroically located his wife and was waiting to take them back, and Lil herself was sitting quietly expecting to leave with "her dress". What could he do? The lady said that was a special price for him 'because of *the situation*'. He put it on his Amex card, handed the fancy boutique bag to Lil and the three of them got back into the Mercedes and returned to the hotel.

On the way back, he received three more anxious texts from his daughter and he replied "I've got her. All well. No need to worry. Just a little confusion on my part. I forgot she was going shopping."

It wasn't enough. The next text from Elle said. "I've booked out on Delta tomorrow. You both need help. We need to bring her back."

At the hotel Lil had her bath and went for a nap.

Hank reflected. He didn't like it. Elle was always so bossy. Talked to him like a child. Lil was just ageing – comes to us all. But he knew he'd taken a big risk bringing her and he hated to be wrong about that. Maybe he was losing it too! He stewed on it. Then he remembered, hell, it was Valentine's night. They were in Paris! What were they supposed to do – lock themselves in with room service? No way! He had a plan and he was sticking to it.

At about six in the evening he woke Lillian and told her

to get dressed up, make-up, jewellery, "The full works honey, like we used to" and to put on the blue dress.

"Am I getting married again?" asked Lil.

Hank ran along with it and said, "You sure are darling, you sure are" and Lil seemed very pleased with this response.

In the cab Lil asked, "Where are we going?" again and again.

Hank tried explaining where the café was, but the answers didn't seem to suit her, so instead he said, "We're going for a date".

In the café they sat under a striped awning with the warmth of overhead heaters keeping off the chilly February air. They could see the Eiffel tower clearly across the Seine. Lillian took off her coat and sat there admiring the silk sapphire weave of her dress. Hank ordered Kir Royales and when the waiter brought the drinks and as they arrived he raised his glass towards her and said "Santé my darling".

"Santé means health in French," replied Lil.

Truth was, she didn't have much conversation anymore and what she did have was pretty disjointed. She seemed in her own world a lot, so he'd kind of got used to spending more time just thinking to himself or observing. He saw a French family eating dinner together, three generations chatting animatedly. It being Valentine's there were a lot of couples out for the evening. A good-looking pair of youngsters couldn't keep their hands off each other. Could he remember those times with Lil? He knew he was hot for her way back then, but he couldn't quite imagine what that really felt like any more. But it didn't matter. They had made a marriage, raised three good kids, seen a bit of the world, made some great buddies and helped some good causes along the way. It had been a life worth living. His Dad would be proud. And all through his adult life there had been Lillian, woven like a silk thread into his very being. He looked across at her. The dress was gorgeous but it sure was too big for her, yet it didn't seem to matter to her – if anything it leant her a kind of radiance and, what was the word, I guess, elegance, yes, she looked elegant. And he just couldn't take on board the idea that he was losing her. They were all wrong, she was just going a bit dotty and god knows we are all like that sometimes. But the text from Elle had hit home hard, had penetrated his stubborn old skin. Lil wasn't right in the head anymore. Heck, more often nowadays Lil wasn't even Lil anymore and sometimes she didn't recognise him. I guess they are all right and I'm stupidly, stubbornly wrong. Wrong to keep pretending. Wrong to bring her to Paris.

What brought him out of his reverie was a sudden wave of chatter and commentary and he looked up to find that the lights on the tower were twinkling and everyone's eyes turned to admire the spectacle. No doubt about it – that is one of the prettiest things you can see. He reached across the table and took hold of Lil's hand. She was absorbed watching the display of lights – she looked quickly at him and he caught a reflection in her eyes, a reflection not just of twinkling lights but of something deeper and more personal, like she was looking right into his soul.

They sat in silence for a few minutes. Then Lil started speaking.

"I remember when we went to Rome and one evening you took me to the Villa d'Este with all those fountains. I had walked so far that day, my feet were tired and sore, and you said take your shoes off and bathe them in one of the fountains, and I did. We watched the sun go down over the hills."

And then she said, "I remember when Michael and Jo-Anne and Elle were little, and we spent Christmas in Vermont and there was an enormous tree, so tall, and we couldn't afford the decorations, so I sat with the kids making our own paper and glitter decorations and we baked gingerbread men and made barley-sugar canes too."

After a few minutes Lillian opened her handbag and without any fuss or fanfare she handed Hank a little bundle. He took it from her, puzzled. He couldn't quite believe what he was seeing. He remembered how, over the years on each visit, Lil had acquired the habit of buying vintage Valentine's postcards. To be frank, he'd found them kind of corny and they were tatty and faded too. Some of them must have dated back to the 20's and 30's, but here they all were, with their cherubs, and little girls with flowers and bonnets, and countless pink hearts. How had she hidden them away and kept them safe all these years? What had possessed her to bring them with her?

Hank recalled how Lil had a kind of notion that each card was a token of distant love and romance, like a silent reminder to us from strangers in the past, as if to say: 'We lived. We loved. Once we were here too'.

He turned them over in his hands now and looked at the old stamps and the fine writing – it was hard to read the French – but you could see words like "Cherie" and "Amour". It wasn't corny at all. How could something so frayed and tired and old suddenly seem so beautiful?

Hank just looked at Lil, in awe. She couldn't remember what she did this morning or even half an hour ago, but she could unearth all these beautiful memories. He could hardly keep from shedding a tear. Was she really back? Or was this some devilish trick of the brain?

Maybe she was back for good. How perfect that would be. He would tell them, 'Paris brought her back to me'.

But Hank had a question he had long been afraid to ask

her, because he was so afraid of the answer. Yet something about the moment made him do it. Ask that terrible question.

"Lil," he said, "What's my name?"

"Don't be silly now," she said, "I know who you are."

"And what's my name?" he asked again.

But Lil said nothing and looked towards the Eiffel Tower as if the magical lights might reappear and bring her an answer.

"You're the very nice man that takes care of me." she said.

Paris would not bring her back. He gazed over at her; okay he knew deep down it wasn't going to be the same, but for now she was still a kind of Lillian, she was still present in his life, just in her own different way, and he still loved her, this version of her. Aren't we all different versions of ourselves at times?

Hank searched for the right thing to say, something that might be special in Lillian's new world.

He said, "You look so beautiful in your blue dress. Will you marry me?"

Lil smiled at him, a shy little girl smile, and she looked down at her diamond engagement ring and her gold band.

"Now you must know that's impossible," she said, "I'm a happily married woman."

# The Breath of Paris

## Present day

*When you write with ink, remember the paper*
*When you turn the page, remember the water in the mill*
*When you drink the water, remember the spring*
*When you find the spring, remember the river*

The coach pulled in to a side street and the guide picked up his microphone.

"Now we will visit the world-famous Paris cathedral of Notre Dame. It will be crowded today so everyone must try to stay close to me. We have forty- five minutes."

Li Ling touched her palms; sweaty. She managed a smile for her uncle and aunt as they got up from their seats, cameras around their necks. Over a roof-top she glimpsed the strange Gothic spires reaching up toward heaven. For a fleeting moment it reminded her of the Tianning temple in Beijing. As her uncle and aunt moved down the coach to get off, Li Ling waited a moment and quickly placed the postcard of the Eiffel Tower on their seats, with her message written on the back:

*I am going to visit a friend. I will be safe. Please don't panic or call the police. I will return tomorrow. I am sorry to cause you upset. Li Ling.*

It unfolded exactly as Shen had described. As the tour group rounded a corner and the cathedral came into view everyone in the party looked up and lifted their phones and cameras. Li Ling held back a little, pretending to adjust the strap of her backpack. Ahead of her she could hear a commotion with some shouting and swearing involving the tour guide. As the confrontation developed Li Ling found herself staring at the backs of the entire coach party.

It felt as if they knew her secret, but they couldn't possibly know. It all seemed so easy that for one moment she hesitated, watching them as they craned their necks forward to get a better view and see what the disturbance was about. Her uncle and aunt were there too, peering over heads to see the cause of the delay. Li Ling simply turned around and started walking quickly in the other direction, putting on her rain-jacket and lifting the hood to cover her jet-black hair. At the next intersection she headed away from the cathedral. Should she run or walk? She felt her heart thumping in her chest. It seemed ready to burst, like the fast-beating heart of the scared rabbit she once held close on a school outing. But with Shen's instructions on her phone she was able to find the little bridge across to the Ile St Louis. Tourists were doing normal things like eating outside cafés, queuing to buy ice creams and taking selfies but still she felt that everyone was staring at her. Her phone started buzzing. Missed call and texts from her uncle. She didn't want to stop to look at it. Instead she switched it off and hurried into the labyrinth of small back streets on the little island and away from the crowds. Outside the security of the coach, without the guide, she felt vulnerable. What did the street-signs mean? What strange pungent smells emerge from the back doors of shops and restaurants. Leaning against an old wooden door, she tried to catch her breath. Despite the fear and the knowledge that there would be a terrible price to pay, she couldn't help but smile and laugh at herself. It was the most exciting thing she had ever done in her nineteen years of life.

In his first semester at the Sorbonne he thought about her often. Of the hundreds of pictures on his phone he had selected the one of her at the Fragrant Hill Festival to be his screen background. There was something wistful in her glance. Her fringe made you focus on her almond shaped eyes. There was a halo of orange and red acer leaves behind her, like a Russian icon. He drew his finger over the smooth glass screen of the phone, remembering the first kiss, the first embrace. What did his father use to say? Beauty is the wisdom of women. Father was smart, sharp in business, a good deal-maker, a talker, always with the right saying. The factory had made them wealthy. Wealthy enough for Shen to be one of the lucky few to attend a new engineering science degree course for Chinese students at the Sorbonne. Bright enough to be selected. They made it clear he was representing his family and his country – a privilege and an honour. He was dutiful and said what they wanted to hear. Emails back to the family reporting on progress with his studies. Conversations with the faculty which he knew would be relayed back to Beijing: yes, he was enjoying the course; yes, he was working hard; yes, he had made friends and no, he did not feel isolated. He didn't mind telling lies if necessary, it was part of the game. He was smarter than they knew, like his father.

Privately it was different. The other foreign students didn't seem that serious about studying. They smoked and drank too much. The food was unappealing – he missed his mother's home-cooking, and he had cravings for sweet-scented dumplings. The smells and sounds of Paris were alien. Beijing was a whole symphony of scents and noises merged into one unified experience which he had known since a child and never questioned. But everything in Paris felt rarefied and separate. The smell of baking bread was cloying, the tree canopy in the park after rain smelled sour, even the cigarette smoke was acrid not sweet. And everywhere he went Li Ling was absent, which made Paris feel lonely and empty.

They had made solemn promises to each other. No messaging. No phone calls. If they could not be together then what use a virtual friendship? He regretted the decision often but knew that when he and Li Ling made a vow it was honoured. When they were sixteen they touched each other's bodies for the first time. What a feeling! Their passion was overwhelming and made even more exquisite by their denial of each other. They doubted that their blissful innocence could survive the torrents of new feelings that besieged them. Yet somehow their bond proved stronger than their ardour and so they made a pact to wait until they married before having sex. Compared to their friends they seemed uncool and old-fashioned but that only made them more determined. As time passed they cherished their sacrifice.

It was a cold night towards the end of the year. Li Ling was sitting at her tiny desk in her room on the campus of Beijing University. She put down her pen, closed the notebook, turned the tiny key in the heart shaped lock and placed it on the shelf behind her folders and textbooks, away from prying eyes. Even a starving country mouse could open the lock, it was so feeble, but there was a ritual sense of privacy about it which made her feel special. Shen had given her the pink and white notebook with the cartoon butterfly on the cover for her 13th birthday. He said he hoped she would write some words about the two of them and keep it as her secret. For six years she had kept the notebook, opening and looking at the pristine pages. Surely any silly schoolgirl could find something to say? But the right words never seemed to come. After a while she came to love the purity of the empty space on the page, left forever open for her imagination to fill. Until Shen left for Paris. Then the empty pages seemed to taunt her. How to find words to describe the pain, the gnawing ache?

*Like the river that longs to be rain,*
*The rain that dreams to be cloud*
*Or the cloud that pines for the ocean*

But she missed him more than that, much more than words could possibly describe. Li Ling, the chatterbox, spoke less and less each day. On a warm autumn morning her proud parents said goodbye to their little canary as she stood on the steps of the university, bearer of a scholarship to study Literature. Then at the next academic break, their precious bird returned mute and burdened with thought.

"I see no light in her eyes", her mother said.

"She is home-sick. She will get over it. She must study hard, she has the gift of a strong mind, I know she will get over it." said her father.

But her mother prevailed.

"She spends too long with her head in books. A bird needs to feel the sun!"

When her mother's brother announced he was taking his wife to Europe for a tour the following spring, Li Ling's mother cajoled and flattered and finally succeeded in persuading them to take their niece with them.

"Let her see the wide world. We Chinese have spent too long looking inwards. It will open her eyes".

Back at university, without her schoolfriends, without Shen, Li Ling poured the pain of her loneliness into study. The scholarship was a precious gift for the child of a struggling family. Honour and expectation demanded the pursuit of academic excellence. Even as her heart was reduced to cinders, so her mind burned brightly. The library became a second home. She went beyond the confines of her curriculum. French literature captured her romantic imagination. In late night sessions she greedily consumed Baudelaire, Balzac, Stendahl, Hugo and Dumas. She was inspired by Rimbaud and Verlaine.

*A book holds a house of gold*

*The wisdom of ages in each word*
*The threads of life in every letter*

With every week that passed, as the grey Paris winter turned to mellow spring, Shen began to open up and enjoy the company of other foreign students, many of whom were studying art and literature. He fell in with a crowd who hung around the cafés and bars off the Canal St Martin or the back streets of the Sorbonne. He began to smoke and drink wine even though the taste was initially unpleasant to him. He began to laugh with his new mates and tell stories, to chat about women on the course and get drunk at parties. He looked less at the image of Li Ling on his phone and he felt guilty about that, and he felt ashamed that he had told his new friends about his childhood love and their pact. They teased him about her. "Shen, Oh Shen, your virgin princess is looking for you on Facebook!" and "Hey Shen, look, here's Li Ling on Tinder!"

He had to grin and take it, wishing he'd kept quiet about her. He saw how juvenile it all seemed in their eyes and gradually in his mind he questioned how long it would go on. Yet strangely Li Ling was the only one with whom he wanted to confide all these ambiguous feelings...if they could just go back to the way things were, all would be well.

Shen spent more time carousing with his intellectual friends and less time studying engineering. He took to wearing black jeans and retro T shirts and grew a thick stubble which he thought made him look more intriguing. For the first time in his life he began to imagine himself as part-European. He dreamed of visiting Berlin and Rome and Bucharest. He pictured himself as the romantic lead in a film noir, drinking schnapps in basement clubs in Amsterdam and taking dreamy-eyed lovers on midnight trains to Istanbul. He began dating a girl and threw himself deep into discovering the thrills of his first proper sexual relationship.

Then, out of the blue, a text came in from Li Ling. He had to read it twice to believe it. She was going to be in Paris, asking how she could meet him! His first thought was that she had broken the pact. How could she? He felt angry and guilty. The pact seemed a puerile idea now, a game dreamed up between two children. What did the past matter when his exciting European adventures beckoned him? But still there came from deep in his heart a swell that was both the memory of love and a nostalgic yearning. Although her arrival had thrown his whole precarious new world off its axis he knew he had to see her. The only question was: how on earth could she escape from the watchful eyes of her chaperones for a night to see him? He confided in his friends, and of course they teased him mercilessly about his lovebird coming to find him. But at the same time, they were amused and intrigued, and together they hatched a plan for Li Ling to have a chance to get away from the shackles of the tour guide.

Li Ling carried on walking, following the instructions Shen had given her. Every now and again she turned to look back, expecting to see her uncle and aunt racing towards her, or the coach screaming down the road in pursuit. As she crossed the Pont de la Tournelle, she glanced back towards Notre Dame. By now they would surely be looking for her? But there was no sign of commotion, nothing. Soon she would be in Shen's arms again! Now this was an adventure worthy of any teenage girl's notebook! But how to describe it all? The exhilaration, alone in a foreign city, the anticipation of romance, the delight in being so rebellious. But these sensations were nothing, nothing compared to the wonderment of seeing Shen, her Shen, standing on the corner of the Boulevard St Germain. He walked towards her with his arms held out, like a scene from a movie. It could only be him, yet he looked so different! His beard, his trendy student clothes, even physically she sensed he had grown bigger, manly, and he walked differently, with a kind of swagger. It almost wasn't him, it almost wasn't Shen.

They hugged each other, awkwardly, but still she felt the butterflies in her stomach and her heart beat faster. They walked in silence for several minutes, holding hands. He led her down little side streets, cutting through university buildings and archways, obviously so familiar to him, but an alien labyrinth to her. Then they began to chat, at first self-consciously, talking over each other in their excitement, but soon they were laughing at the sheer craziness of being together again in Paris.

Li Ling noticed that his sense of humour had changed, now it seemed sardonic and his manner of speaking more mature and measured. It was different, it was not exactly the Shen she remembered or expected. This new Shen was still attractive - but disarming. He had become foreign, as strange and beguiling as the unknowable streets of this foreign city.

She had imagined that they would soon be alone in his cosy room, catching up on all the moments they had missed since he left. She would share some of her poetry, they would drink a glass of French wine, and lean back together on his student bed, with his arm around her shoulders.

But to her disappointment Shen insisted that they meet his friends first. He was quite insistent, so she felt obliged to go along with his plan.

"They helped me plot your escape, so they are all desperate to meet you – you can't not see them!" he said.

Shen and his student buddies liked to gather in the Café Lautrec, a coffee-house cum wine bar in a back street near the square Robert-Montagne. At first Li Ling was the natural object of attention and curiosity and Shen tried to ensure she was introduced to everyone, but still she felt self-conscious and shy. They teased Shen and joked about their latest prank and repeated the story of her escape to every new friend who joined the table. Eventually there must have been ten or twelve of them clustered around in groups, beer bottles and wine glasses stacking up on the scrubbed wooden table. She could see Shen become animated as the conversation became louder and he drank more wine.

The more the gathering became rowdy the more Li Ling faded more into the background, taking occasional sips of white wine. She studied the people and the decor of the café. With its rather tired Alphonse Mucha posters of famous dancers and music halls, and its Tiffany lamps it was almost exactly how she had imagined a Paris café would look and feel, from her reading of 19th century French romantic authors. The boy sitting next to her had some books of poetry on top of his bag. Li Ling smiled at him and picked one up. It was called "The White Room" by Jules Moncrieff. She had never heard of him; but then her idea of modern poetry was T.S.Eliot. It looked interesting and she sat for a while reading the first few poems.

She would like to have spoken about poetry, even about her own poems, but there was no chance because they all spoke French in a fast, colloquial way, and she couldn't follow the conversations. She wanted to leave but she didn't have the courage to ask Shen. She tried to catch his eye, but he was engrossed in a debate with a fair-haired girl who looked somehow Scandinavian. Did he have a girl-friend here Li Ling wondered? Unable to escape, she sat back and shyly observed their behaviour, trying not to look too much at Shen. They were all so different looking - boys with beards or ponytails, girls with long straight fine blonde hair, girls with tanned skin and dark hair tied up with a scarf. It was all so...diverse...they all seemed so confident in themselves. And the strangest one of all, thought Li Ling, was Shen, her boy, her teenage sweetheart, who now seemed to blend in with the others. Finally, with a lot of banter and elaborate goodbyes people started to leave and Li Ling sensed the end of her ordeal and the chance to be alone with Shen.

She had already decided that she would make love to him that night. Long before seeing the Scandinavian looking girl fawning over him, long before the wine bar, long before Paris even, she had decided that it would happen the next time they met. She just hadn't expected it to be this way.

Back in his room they sat together on the edge of his bed, fumbling for words, starting conversations at the same time then stopping to let the other speak, followed by nervous laughter. Shen started to ramble on about his friends, his life, how she would love it in Paris, how he felt free and a sense of awakening. Then he would backtrack and apologise if she felt awkward and how it had been a mistake to take her to the café. Li Ling wanted to hear it all, to have every detail brought out, to share all the moments like they used to. Most of all she wanted to understand how he felt about her, about her arriving unannounced. But it was obvious the wine had gone to his head and this was not the moment, so she pressed her fingers against his lips and put her hand around the back of his neck, pulling him towards her, falling backwards onto the bed.

Many years later, looking back, she realised that it could never have been as she had imagined or hoped. She was naïve and innocent, she dreamed of tender sweet moments, of a euphoria that would do justice to the precious innocence of their shared youth. But it was awkward. Although whispering endearments to her and repeating her name Shen seemed mindless and mechanical. They fumbled with clothes and limbs until he moved his hand between her legs and touched her, not roughly but not gently either, but matter of factly, as if she was an animal being prepared for mating. She was amazed to feel so wet with desire, so that as he entered her she felt only a short moment of pain followed by deep, delicious waves of unexpected pleasure. As he lay on top of her moving faster inside her she looked over his shoulder at the window where streetlight was casting a pale wash across the ceiling and she imagined looking down upon herself, here in a strange room in a strange city. She saw her legs wrapped around Shen's back, saw her dark hair on the pillow and her eyes full of wonder and lust and fear. And then it came into her mind with a dread realisation that he knew what he was doing - this was not his first time. How silly she had been to think they would both share their first time together, as if from some romantic fairy story.

Shen's breathing became more urgent and his thrusts deeper until he groaned and suddenly pulled out of her and lay on top of her, still rocking back and forth against her, kissing her neck until he rolled to her side and lay still and silent except for his breathing which gradually slowed and quietened. She whispered his name. "Shen". Again, more loudly. "Shen!" and touched his hair, but he remained asleep.

She remembered lying still, thinking she must not wake him, but then she began to feel cold and afraid. Could she become pregnant even if he pulled out of her? Why hadn't they even thought about it? She pulled a sheet over her and stared upwards, up to the ceiling, above the ceiling to the rooftops of Paris, up to the clouds and the moon and stars, and suddenly she felt alone and very small.

Did she sleep at all? She wasn't sure. Her thoughts and emotions were a scrambled mess. Standing at the window she looked down at Shen, still in a deep sleep, and she looked around at his room. Did she even know this boy with his framed posters of obscure bands, his keyboard in the corner and his books and essay papers scattered untidily across an old desk? As dawn light crept in at the window Li Ling slipped on her clothes and with her shoes in her hands she tiptoed to the door and hurried down the stairs.

Paris was just beginning to raise itself from a slumber. A streetcleaner drove his mini vehicle around the edges of gutters and pavements. As she found her way back to St Germain a few early commuters headed down the steps to the metro and an empty bus passed by. There had been rain overnight and the pavements and slate rooftops glistened in the early light.

A glow came from the window of a boulangerie. Hungry and needing directions Li Ling went to open the door even though the hanging sign said "Fermé". The owner at the back of the shop pointed at the sign. Li Ling raised her hands together in the universal sign of supplication and smiled as sweetly as one could for someone who is lost in a city and lost in love. Something about her waif like face must have struck a chord because the man opened the door six inches and demanded to know what she wanted. In her broken French Li Ling asked for directions to get a taxi and could he open so she could buy some bread? Begrudgingly the man gave her some directions in rapid French which she didn't catch, but his fingers had gestured across the boulevard. She fished in her purse for some money but before she could ask how much the man shoved a freshly baked baguette through the door. With a shrug of the shoulders and an 'Allez!' he closed the door and went back to his morning's work.

The bread felt like the best thing she had ever eaten. It was warm and sweet and tasted of goodness. It filled her stomach with courage and she walked on, heading roughly where she thought she had started the day before, near the river, where she hoped to find a taxi. But the prospect of the reception that would await her back at the hotel came chillingly into her thoughts. Her parents would be told. For the rest of the tour she would probably be hand-cuffed to her uncle and aunt! Or confined to the hotel. How much should she tell them? She would be disgraced in their eyes. And all for what? She nibbled on the baguette and kept walking, until with relief she saw the imposing outline of the cathedral rising out of the river mist and on the quayside the unmistakeable glowing signs on the roofs of taxis, as their drivers stood around, smoking and chatting, waiting for the rush hour.

Putting off the ominous journey back to the hotel for a few minutes, Li Ling crossed the bridge and stood looking down at the river, trying to collect her thoughts. Victor Hugo had said:

*"Breathing Paris preserves the soul".*

She tried to breathe it in one more time. What did it taste like, this breath of Paris, at this moment, alone at dawn? Loneliness and sadness of course, and disappointment, and disillusionment? And the bitter sweetness of first loves' promises broken. But the sun will rise again soon, like Baudelaire's poem Le Soleil, she thought, it's warm fingertips reaching down grand avenues and poor side-streets, gradually revealing all the lusts and longing of a great city. Li Ling looked over the ripples of the Seine, tinged with the silvery apricot ribbons of dawn light. And today, all these people rising from their beds, dressing and preparing for the unknown joys and sorrows of the day ahead, is it all a kind of blind bravery? For the first time in her life she felt a sense of being part of a grand drama, as if she was playing a role in Victor Hugo's Paris, in the footsteps of Fantine and Cosette.

In the warmth of the taxi, Li Ling lay back against the soft seat, closed her eyes and let the experiences of the last day and night imprint on her memory before she dared to switch her phone back on.

Much later, after the recriminations and the punishments, after the return to Beijing, she poured out her soul onto the pages of the butterfly notebook, tender word after word, soaring line after line, until it was filled with the breath and the whisper of Paris.

*My words are sent like autumn swallows*
*Guided by heaven's map they fly to you*
*Close your book of studies Shen*
*And let the stars into your eyes*

# The Chemistry of Love

## Present day

"No cases for the hold today Mr Sullivan?"

"Nope, just one overnight and I'm flying back tomorrow"

"One night in Paris, how I envy you – any special plans?"

At this point Chris paid a little more attention to the check-in clerk. She was kind of his type, neat, well-groomed, not too much make-up. There was no doubting the sharpness of the uniform added to her appeal.

"Actually, I'm giving a lecture. I've just had a book published", he said.

"Oh really – anything I would have heard of?" She made eye contact and smiled at him as she handed over his boarding card. Feeling rather pleased with himself, Chris replied, with false modesty.

"Oh, I doubt it; it's called the Chemistry of Love."

"The Chemistry of Love. Sounds intriguing. I will definitely have to look that one up!"

"Well, it's not exactly a best-seller, more what you'd call popular science."

He smiled back at her, took the boarding card and headed for departures. Later, as the plane reached cruising height, he sat back and reflected on the last few years. This had always been his habit when flying. A chance to just quietly think about all that had happened and where his life might lead next – perhaps it was the awareness of his own fragile mortality, sitting in a giant metal cigar tube, thirty-five thousand feet above the English countryside, which prompted these feelings.

His divorce from Clare seemed distant now - was it really four years since the final parting? In that time the pain had been successfully numbed, numbed by all the things he'd crammed into his life. A change of job – moving from research science to the academic world. Not the classic career path, but it had reinvigorated him, and he had to admit that the book would never have happened if he had still been working in the labs.

He continued running through his mental check-list, while from his window he watched the English Channel and then the coast of France slide under the plane like images on a computer screen. What else? The new apartment had been a success – without all of Clare's stuff and her offbeat tastes in decoration he had been able to plan and create a whole interior world that suited him perfectly. White walls, naturally; leather sofas, chrome lamps, oak flooring. On one wall a giant 60's Marvel comics poster and on the other a 68" super flat screen TV. Near the window, a gleaming steel and glass office desk with his 27" iMac enthroned on top, his command centre. A Bose wireless sound system ready to play whatever his mood demanded, his digital collection categorised and tagged to perfection. Crisply ordered on the bookshelves sat what was, admittedly, a somewhat eclectic collection; heavy academic reading, popular science (a more recent interest), wartime history, just about every Le Carré, and then older stuff from his University and school days, there was even some Keats and Shelley in there. Even though it lacked structure he flattered himself that it created an intriguing first impression. And, of course, his growing collection of vinyl albums, stored strictly in alphabetic order by artist surname or band name. Definitely a talking point; though now he came to think of it he hadn't had that many conversations about it.

The new car was a bonus too, an Audi of course, a TT Quattro, in white with black leather. So beautifully engineered, so precise in every little detail. So faithful. What else? Of course, his bike. A Cannondale Super Six, a symphony in black carbon fibre. And on the road, mile after mile, he became fitter, leaner in body and mind and somehow purified, leaving the emotional distress of his divorce in the swirling slipstream behind him.

All these things Chris Sullivan, a handsome, sensitive and cautious man who knew he was the wrong side of thirty-five, built up carefully as barricades to set against the past and to afford protection in the future.

As the plane banked and prepared for its descent into Paris his reverie shifted towards the reason for his visit. The lecture, the book – he still couldn't quite believe it had happened and here he was almost a minor celebrity. When friends asked about the genesis of the book he explained that he had been contemplating a more creative role for some time and this was the natural and logical outcome. But deep down he knew that it had simply come out of nowhere - a totally random series of events. One day he was deep into chemical analysis, researching Oxytocin and Vasopressin receptors and the next day, well not literally, but actually about eighteen months after he joined the Research Faculty at the University, a publisher had seen him as a guest on TV (had he been chosen as the token eye-candy of the scientific community?) talking about bio-chemical changes when we fall in love. Evidently, they had some kind of eureka moment because it was shortly after that he got the phone call. He thought it might be a joke, but no, it was a commissioning editor from a publishing house calling, would he consider writing something for a wider audience?

For some time he felt conflicted about the proposal – this was lightweight fodder compared to the rigours of his research. How would it play in his career? It wasn't the standard route and it certainly would not receive much approval from his academic peers. But his friends had egged him on and told him to go for it, and the publisher's PR exec charmed him with talk of TV interviews and potential royalties. Vanity.

The plane touched down and he took a cab to his hotel near the Palais Royale. The book was evidently selling quite well, and the publishers were keen to get as much marketing value out of him while the wave of interest was still rolling. Out of the blue they had asked him to give a talk at their 50$^{th}$ anniversary celebrations in Paris where he would be sharing the bill with numerous other authors. Checking into his room he felt strangely nervous – there would be other non-science authors to mingle with. What would they be like? Art and history authors drinking champagne and gushing eloquently to their sycophantic and pretentious publishing cohorts? He feared he would be well out of his comfort zone. He hung up his suit and spare shirt, placed his toiletries next to the wash basin and stored his case in the cupboard. He hooked into the Wi-Fi and checked his email. He didn't know what to do next, so he read the hotel welcome guide and set up the TV and radio alarm clock. From the open window the lonely burble of traffic and the wail of distant sirens were suddenly broken by a call on his mobile.

"Chris, hi! It's Judy... you're here! Did you have a good flight? Is everything OK?" Before he had a chance to reply she had invited him to join her and other attendees for dinner after the reception. "It will be fun – see you just before we start, say 6.30!" she chirped.

He wondered what it took to always sound so irrepressibly cheerful.

There must have been seventy or more at the reception. Although he didn't know anyone other than Judy, his PR contact, he mingled as best he could, feeling slightly out of place in the glittering mélange of writers, agents, editors and publicists.

Much later, in the early hours of the morning, lying awake in bed, he looked back and tried to make sense of what had happened that evening. No doubt the champagne must have played a part, reducing his social inhibitions, distorting his perspective. Was an uncontrollable pattern taking shape from the moment he joined the other guests? Or from the moment he stepped onto the plane? He asked himself again and again when he had first seen her. Was it across the room during the reception? Had some microscopic neural pathway lit up in his mind like a beacon? Otherwise what could explain the sense of déjà vu, the sense of pre-destined recognition that he experienced when he was introduced to her at the dinner?

"Eliza. But call me Elly if you like."

"How's that spelled?" he'd asked. What a dumb question - as if he was going to make a note on his phone.

"Eliza. E L I Z A."

There was a momentary pause when their eyes met, and then she jumped right in and saved his embarrassment. "I'm surprised we don't have those badges you usually get at these dos. Actually, my name is spelled wrongly on the guest list anyway, so you should just feel free to spell it anyway you like. We are in Paris aren't we, you may as well add a couple of accents while you're at it!" Then, in a stage whisper, she said, "I'll tell you a secret. My name is not even supposed to be on the list – I'm the last-minute replacement for someone much more clever" she joked. She had a lilting way of speaking, and he noted her soft Irish accent and the smile in her voice.

"That's how I feel all the time," Chris said, and she laughed at that and as she laughed he noticed her shoulders gave a little tilt forwards and then she would straighten up and the light would catch her hair and her eyes shone with a kind of joyful mischief as she sipped from her glass.

To begin with he tried hard to be engaging and attentive and asked her question after question, knowing how to play this part of the game. And her answers all rolled together in a teasing, rather whimsical way as if she was mocking him a little. He asked about her childhood in Ireland, what was it like to be a teenager in Dublin and she was off like a practised story-teller with her accent sounding more noticeable now as she reminisced in a free-flowing, champagne induced soliloquy.

"Well and what kind of man are you to ask a Dublin girl a question like that? You know my father warned me about men like you! But I've learned to take my chances . . . anyway did you know that you could fetch oysters right out of the river all those years ago . . . my grandpa showed me where to look and we'd wade out and stare through his special box with the glass window until you could see the little beauties nestling under your feet . . . now that is not your average childhood so it isn't . . . "

In return he started to tell her about his science background and his book, but hardly had he got going when they were invited to pile into taxis and head out for dinner with a group of about twelve. Soon they were sitting inside a glamourous restaurant decked out with wooden panelling, painted mirrors and scenes from ocean liners in the 1930's. One of those places that manages to evoke memories of Paris from long ago. As luck would have it he and Eliza were seated opposite each other and as she chatted with the others Chris was able to look over the shoulders of his fellow diners and beyond where he studied the theatrical performance on display. The maître d', a small man with a droopy moustache, was like the stage director or an orchestra conductor, greeting arrivals with aplomb, sending discreet signals here and there to his waiters, having a quiet word with his regular customers. Looking through the enormous glass windows at the front of the restaurant you could see the soft fading light of a spring evening wash over the streets like an aquarelle. The dinner wasn't as formal as he'd imagined, everyone was relaxed and enjoying the flow of conversation and plentiful wine. He leaned back, observing Eliza closely, but without risking a long stare. Were her eyes hazel he wondered and was she maybe late thirties? He noticed the fine tracery of lines around her eyes and mouth and a little slackness under the jaw and the prettiness of a few freckles and the way the little lines creased near the bridge of her nose when she laughed. He thought, yes late thirties, and that would explain her mentioning an ex when the inevitable "marriage and kids" questions arose. But she was so girlish too, so vivacious but in a self-effacing way. It was hard to define what he felt. Having paid dutiful attention to their neighbours at the table they felt safe to return to each other and talk again.

Still Eliza smiled and laughed when she spoke; of riotous teenage years in Dublin, of giving up her job in sales to come to London to study her first love, fine art, of having no money, of life being just unexpected and amazing and here we all are in Paris, and she's helped to edit a book about Manet and well, who'd have thought it!

Just when he thought he could go on all evening listening to her and discreetly studying her, she said, "Now then just wait a second here; I see what you've been doing you naughty man and here's moi with a brain full of champagne and there's you, sorry tu, probably making all your mental science notes like I'm the specimen, like I'm half-decent material for your next book. I know what you scientists are like, tell me I'm not right Christopher!?" He knew she was teasing but it came so suddenly and was awkwardly close to the truth that for a few moments he felt at a loss for words, then he blushed and finally recovered himself, but she saw his embarrassment and said, "Oh me oh my please forgive me Chris I hope I haven't offended you, I'm just rattling away and I'm just too excited to be here and in the company of writers such as yourself. I'll shut up now I promise. Your turn to speak, so now tell me all about the book."

Chris took a deep breath.

## THE CHEMISTRY OF LOVE

"OK well, basically, I've spent many years studying the science behind physical attraction. It's part of what you might call psycho-biology. I did a lot of work in labs looking at dopamine; it's one of the systems that govern the brain's response to attraction and arousal and so on. So, then I switched to the University and I've been leading a new study looking at prairie voles . . . yes really . . . trust me . . . prairie voles do exist, and it turns out they're quite important. I know it sounds weird and you're picturing a bunch of crazy white-coated nerds with their lab rats but here's the thing: the prairie voles actually mate for life – really! And when you study the chemical triggers it's quite astounding what's going on; it's all to do with Oxytocin and Vasopressin receptors. So essentially to try and explain it what we're looking at are the neuro transmitters and the bio-mechanics, what parts of the brain are engaged when we fall in love with someone and what does that tell us about ourselves and about being human."

"You mean it's not just stardust and roses and romantic music then?" Eliza said, with a half-smile and a teasing glance.

He grinned. "Whatever works for you of course, but here's the thing, all of us are pre-programmed to run a series of neuro-chemical reactions when something or I should say someone pulls the trigger. It's as if there is a phial of chemicals sitting in a corner of your brain marked 'Only break this in case of potential mating opportunity".

"Mating opportunity!? Well you are one of the last of the great romantics, aren't you?!" she laughed, with her eyebrows raised fetchingly.

But it was too late to stop now. To his surprise Chris found himself in full flow, describing the scientific studies, the evidence and the next piece of research he had planned. She was listening intently, resting her jaw in her hand and smiling occasionally when he became animated. He stopped to ask her if he was boring her.

She said, "Not at all and you know what, you kind of remind me of my father, but in a good way, he was a lecturer."

Chris wasn't sure if this comment was intended as a compliment or not, but he pressed on regardless. "Between you and me the book is not the same thing as my research, it's just a piece of popular science, and it's been edited to reach a less technical audience. It's as if my scientific work has been decorated, not decorated with a medal but I mean like some kind of fairy cake! And sometimes I fear I've sold my soul to the devil," he whispered conspiratorially.

He took a long slug of wine and sat back, hardly believing where he was and that he had just been so candid with a woman he hardly knew.

It was Eliza's turn to talk, and after a pause she said.

"Well I don't think you've sold out at all, I think you've

just walked in a new direction and that's what life is for, for goodness sake. I admire you for doing that. The thing is Chris, I don't know much about neural pathways and such and I do understand what you're saying, but for me, well, when I think about love and all that stuff it's like comparing the Renaissance artists with say Picasso or Chagall."

"How do you mean?" said Chris.

"Well, the early painters kind of painted what they saw in great detail, I mean they didn't even know how to convey three dimensions to begin with so everything was kind of flat. Whereas when we get to the 20th century painters like Braque and Picasso started to show the world as always moving and changing. You know you can't pin it down, there's always this flux in the story like all the elements are essentially random, you know like Picasso's portraits of women where the parts of the face and body are mixed up like jigsaw pieces."

"And what has that got to do with love?"

"Well I guess what I believe is that you can't prescribe it and maybe it is a lot of chemicals rushing around but surely there could be endless permutations or at least you have to recognise, maybe, that it's not the science so much as the story – kind of like The Life of Pi, you know? It's down to you to choose the best story."

Chris smiled at her and thought to himself how deftly

she had just summed her view up in a few words. It was charming and endearing and unsettling all at the same time. In his world there were always more uncertainties to be discovered and pinned down, like Lepidoptera in wooden drawers. Yet in one way she was right because all the research ultimately pointed to the science of human attraction being subject to the vagaries of genetics and environmental conditioning. The chemistry was the same, or the ingredients were, but the way one person falls in love and the triggers they experience had endless permutations.

"Do you like art?" Eliza asked him.

"Actually, yes I do. I think I have pretty eclectic tastes though. I like Hockney and 60's pop art, but I also have a soft spot for Holman Hunt. Come to think of it you have a sort of pre-Raphaelite look about you," he joked.

"Pre-Raphaelite! So do you see me as your Ophelia, Mr Hamlet?! All that drowning in the river - scary. Actually, I like them too, but I'm surprised a scientist likes them, I mean they are quite romantic with a capital R, are they not?"

"I suppose so, I just love the detail and the layers of meaning that you can uncover . . ," he trailed off as he noticed activity around them.

People were leaving the restaurant now. Instead of finishing his rambling opinions about art Chris said, "I hope we can see each other again. Can I have your number?" and he handed her his pen, a Parker Classic from the 70's.

"Snazzy pen! I was going to text you or at least scribble on a scrap of paper, but I think this pen deserves better", and she produced a postcard from within her bag. "Found time to go to the Petit Palais today – wonderful impressionists - and bought a few souvenirs! You can have one for being so nice", she said as she wrote her number on the back of the card and handed it to Chris.

There was much banter and bisous as the guests parted with good luck wishes for the next day for the speakers and Judy the PR came over to Chris and said, "Well I see you two have met – the rumour going round is that you must have known each other in a former life, the way you were in such deep conversation!"

And then, to his astonishment, Eliza said, quite matter-of-factly, "I think perhaps we do know each other from a former life."

Chris thought that he would never have the nerve to say something like that. It was disarming and alluring, and he felt confused and could not explain his thoughts to himself. To think they might have met in a former life or even in the same life was ridiculous, but still he found what she said touched him and the feeling was like an endorphin rush. He could feel himself blushing.

After leaving the restaurant they found themselves

walking along random streets until they reached the embankment above the Seine, not talking, but they were arm in arm now and it seemed natural, not flirtatious, it was just the thing all Parisians do, wasn't it? They watched the bateaux-mouches glide under the bridges and caught little drifts of tour guide commentary in the air. Late night taxis, their meters glowing like fireflies, were taking people to their homes as the city seemed to sigh at the end of another day.

"Well. Some of us have talks to give tomorrow morning," said Chris, trying to be nonchalant, "I guess I really should be getting back. We'll share a cab yeah?"

"Of course, you must," said Eliza quietly, and glanced at him with a look that he found hard to interpret.

Now the buoyant mood of the evening that had carried him along happily on its current was beginning to wear off and the memories of their conversations were bubbling under the surface of his thoughts like fragments of unsorted debris. Inside him he felt an old anxiety swell up like some deep-sea creature emerging from a lair, feelings he had thought were drowned were coming back to life. He needed to lie down and sleep and start tomorrow afresh and have time to think about everything.

They didn't speak in the taxi, each content to look out of the window at the lights and late-night revellers. The taxi dropped Eliza off first at her hotel. Their good-night parting was clumsy. "I'll call you!" he shouted after her as the door closed.

There was no doubt that he found her fascinating and attractive and he desired her. He had briefly imagined that the evening would end up with the two of them in his room, making love and getting up in the night to look at the moonlight over the rooftops of Paris. But now on his return to the hotel, under the bright lights of the lobby the adrenaline and alcohol were creating mixed emotions.

That night he couldn't get to sleep for hours. His mind was a whirlwind spinning their conversations round and round, over and over. He tried to rationalise things. Two divorcees, in Paris, champagne and fine wine – it was only nature doing what it does when there is mutual physical attraction. He tossed and turned, and his mind ran on again. Had she really teased him about his book? Had he bored her? Was her hair really that black, glossy like a raven, like an Irish raven?

He woke late and dashed into the shower, nervous tension building already about his talk. He told himself it wasn't like an academic paper; there would be no reviews and tricky questions. Just "fans and some of our friends in publishing" according to Judy.

Fighting off a slight hangover, he drank coffee and

juice and studied his laptop slides, making mental notes for his talk. It took all his discipline to put aside in his mind the events of the previous evening, but now, unlike when he went to bed, he felt in control of the schedule and able to organise his thoughts. Just once did he pause and look out of the window to gaze at the Paris roof-tops, wondering if she was in her room somewhere across town doing the same thing. From his jacket pocket he retrieved the card with her number. The image was a portrait of Sarah Bernhardt, a stunning painting of the subject reclining languidly on a red velvet couch. For a moment he thought he could see a resemblance to Eliza, the dark hair and pale skin – a kind of wild beauty. She had written her number and her name, in capitals, teasing him. He said her name aloud, 'Eliza', and it made him smile. Should he? Could he? Or would he leave it as a pleasant memory to add to many others in his life, filed away in an archive drawer, to bring out and study from time to time.

With his heart starting to beat faster, he picked up his phone and tapped in the number. After three rings it went to voicemail and he listened to her cheery message:

"Hi, you've reached Eliza Brennan. As you can tell I can't answer your call right now but leave me a message and I'll be sure to call right back. Byee!"

For a few seconds he debated whether to leave a

message, then decided against it and quickly hung up. It was a sign. He was being a damn fool. 'Just leave it, you don't need any complications right now', he thought to himself. He closed the laptop and prepared to head down to the conference room.

Sitting at the front of the hall he listened as Judy gave an embarrassingly eulogistic introduction to his talk. He hoped no-one from the academic community would be here to see him squirm. His eyes took in the room where perhaps eighty to a hundred guests were seated, more than he had expected. "It's a good turn-out," Judy whispered before leaving him alone at the podium.

He gave it his best shot but looking back he knew he had been below par, a combination of alcohol and lack of sleep, he supposed. Not only that, but at random moments he lost his train of thought and had to pause briefly and look down to his notes. Nevertheless, he had produced some amusing slides and cracked a few witty asides and the audience seemed genuinely responsive.

"So, in conclusion, there have been many attempts to define the unique feelings we experience when falling in love, from the songs of Solomon, to the troubadours and the medieval obsession with courtly love, to the poetry of Byron and the Hollywood romance. But now, thanks to scientific research we can see what is really happening in our bodies and minds, we understand empirically the reactions that will take place when these moments occur. So, when two people meet and fall in love and they say 'there was chemistry between us', well now you know there really was! Thank you so much for listening."

Chris was relieved to hear the level of applause and felt a surge of confidence at having completed the talk with no major mishaps. There were a few routine questions, then a lull. He closed his laptop. Then, just as he could begin to picture himself on the plane en route back to London, there was another question, this time from right at the back of the audience. He couldn't quite see the person asking the question, but a female voice said, "I enjoyed your talk, thank you. But I was just wondering . . . so, do these theories mean that the idea of falling in love with someone on a first meeting is inconceivable?"

Chris's brain processed the question and began to swiftly construct what a suitable answer would be. But a millisecond later those thoughts were drowned in a tsunami of doubt and confusion. Because, could it be, yes it had to be her voice, and now he caught sight of her and could connect the voice to the figure with black hair and red coat, as she sat right there in the back row.

It was only a few seconds but in that brief time it felt like a chasm had opened before him. He was free-falling and grasping out, hoping for any kind of instinct to take hold. After what seemed an eternity he re-gathered his faculties sufficient for his inner man of science, the doubt-free voice of reason, to come to his rescue. "I believe you have to put that expression and that, if I may say so, quintessentially romantic concept, into some kind of scientific context. My book is about what happens to all people, to everyone, so in that sense there is nothing unique about the experience, which would imply that, well . . ." He was stumbling a little now but pressed on, "I think it would be hard to take that notion very seriously."

He was mumbling, and his answer tailed off as he looked down at his notes and then looked quizzically in her direction, half-hoping he'd made a mistake about her identity. People in the audience were murmuring and their curiosities were roused - they sniffed blood, this wasn't part of the programme, something wasn't quite right.

He noticed her stand up and squeeze along the row to the aisle where she paused and stared at him. 'Good grief, it *is* Eliza, and what the hell is she doing and what on earth is going on here' were all he could think as the room fell silent, half of the audience looking at her and half at him.

She stood buttoning her coat, looked straight at him and said "So, Mr Sullivan, shall I take your answer as a Yes?", and she turned towards the door.

He stood at the podium, frozen, unhinged. Then, from some primal recess of his mind, like a child speaking its first words he opened his mouth and said, "Wait!"

She half turned back towards him, with one hand on the door handle. Now the audience was gripped - this was like a bonus feature, a mini-drama to round off the main event. He felt light-headed. Was there some lesson, some instruction he could summon up from his past, something instinctive to carry him through this moment. He stepped down from the stage and walked along the aisle towards her. A hundred heads turned to follow him. He said, "I'm wrong. Somewhere I've gone wrong."

He walked towards the rear of the room until he reached her. "What I mean is the answer to your question, for me, personally, the answer to your question is . . .", and taking her hand in his, he said, "the answer to your question is . . . yes, I mean no, it's not inconceivable."

People in the audience started murmuring to their neighbours, trying to work out the implications of this little tableau; and then someone felt the instinct to clap as if this was a better way to end his talk and the clapping rippled quietly across the room with what felt like a kind of spontaneous pleasure.

With this applause echoing in their ears Chris and Eliza left the room, their faces flushed. Without speaking they walked out of the lobby and down the hotel steps past the uniformed doorman, moving at a faster pace along the busy pavements and only pausing to stop and look at each other when it seemed they had put some physical distance between themselves and the hotel, as if they needed an urgent escape, having perhaps stolen something precious.

Half a block up the Rue St Honoré they turned into a quiet side road and stood together, holding hands and looking at each other and up at the buildings and the sky swirling around them. On the corner was a small park and they stopped to sit on a bench and said to themselves in their minds to be calm and try to behave like adults.

At first there seemed no need for words or no words that would come, so they sat slightly apart, staring ahead, collecting their thoughts, until eventually Eliza turned to Chris and said, "So, Christopher Sullivan, back in the room there, you were saying?" and she moved a little towards him, looking him deeply in the eye with a quizzical expression, half-smiling, half-questioning.

His heart beat faster. The directness of her look brought him back again to the intense reality of this unexpected but thrilling moment, conscious that this could be the start of a great unplanned experiment. He was on the brink, just holding on, knowing that he could still back away, aware of a sense of time and place unexplored, of a story awaiting the telling, but fearful too, as if the anarchists were loose in the lab and all the animals were being released and all his caged feelings would be untamed and feral again.

How long did that moment last? A few seconds in which time seemed to lose its meaning. A few seconds for him to notice all over again the glossy dark sheen of her hair, the hazel-grey, hazel-brown eyes, the indentations and tiny flaws in her skin and the perfect delicate creases around her mouth; the fullness of her lips, and the milky whiteness of her hands and the green painted bench where they sat together in a park in Paris, and the pinkness of the cherry blossom branches overhanging and the sound of schoolchildren laughing in a distant playground. And all these sounds and sensations were intensely vivid and pressed on his mind like fresh wet imprints glistening with promise and potential.

What was to say or to do? How to act when there was only the absence of control and the whirling chaos of untrusted, untried emotions waiting below the precipice? And yet the way forward was calling out to him louder and more urgently.

As he leans in close to her face he can see in the shine of her eye the reflections of the azure sky and the cherry blossom, and he knows deep within his soul that there is only one gesture, one sublimely imperfect-yet-perfect way for this moment to resolve, out of all the infinitesimal chemical combinations that could occur, that this first kiss and these feelings are uniquely theirs, and theirs alone, forever.

# Les Bouquinistes

## Le Marais, present day

A good start this morning. Finally got the knack of the rusty key and the weird upwards door handle to lock the apartment! Those stairs are dark and a bit creepy, but the hallway has some exquisite old patterned tiles. There's a pungent smell of newly mopped wet disinfectant coming from the basement, so I don't linger inside. The massive wooden blue door clunks shut behind and a bright Paris Spring morning is right here waiting just for me. A skip in my stride. Sparrows are chirruping in the trees and a very old man is strolling along the edge of the pavement. I can smell the sweet yet acrid aroma of his cigarette smoke, his funny little bulldog plods along behind him. Mouth-watering smells of baking as I pass the boulangerie and to a table at my "local" café. Dazzling reflections of polished zinc, aromas of freshly ground coffee masking traffic fumes and Paris drains. My new suede boots, impractical heels I know, but hey I'm walking the streets of Paris (how do these French women walk everywhere in heels?), and my new scarf, Longchamp...over one hundred Euros, ouch, but to die for and I deserve it, right? I feel good. I sip my coffee. I pretend to read Le Figaro. I'm in France. I'm fifty years old, but I feel alive. It's all going to be OK.

That was just this morning, so what changed? It's like slipping or skating from one kind of consciousness to another. What seemed rock solid now feels fragile.

I wanted to see the bouquinistes. You can't go to Paris and not see the bouquinistes, they said. Even Luke had been to them (without me, on his "business" trip, but was it all business? Ha!) and anyway what does he know of books if they're not about software and new business paradigms?

Maybe I should not have Googled 'Paris bouquinistes' before I set off. You know, I think sometimes knowledge gets in the way. I mean, they've been here for literally centuries, since before the revolution even. It's humbling. And it is *so* picturesque with the quay and the river and their old green stalls and all the book covers and the characters...it's pure theatre. But thanks to the great God Internet, I had pre-conceptions, and they got in the way of my appreciation. Then I tried to take a picture and the vendor got shirty with me. 'No photos' he said, tut-tutting at me.

What's his problem? So then I figured I was just being a cheap tourist and I should put the camera away and just like, take it all in. And you know what? He did me a favour with his "No photos" rule. I relaxed. I loved it.

Diane, you would love it too – all these fabulous vintage novels and Vogue covers and old comic book posters. There's this smell of old paper and musty leather, like the books you once found in your grandpa's attic. Some of the sellers are real types, they have this haughty attitude, sitting smoking Gauloises and generally ignoring the browsers. And guess what? You know Charlie is studying French literature...well I found an early volume of Proust, part of La Recherche du Temps Perdu, not leather, but a treasure of a hardback with gorgeous marbled inners and gilded edges. Sixty-five euros! *Mon dieu*! He probably ripped me off but who cares. So, I'm browsing in this one stall. You know how browsing books and vinyl records is one of those things that you do, and you can just lose yourself in it? Anyway, I become aware of this guy glancing at me and he says something like 'I *lurve* zee old books', but with a smoochy French accent of course! What is it with that accent!?

Who am I talking to? Diane? Myself? My conscience? But I want to hold this thought for a while because, because he was good looking with his leather coat and his scarf. Only the French men can get away with the scarf like that and seem cool. And he had a kind of quiet, honest confidence, a weathered face and bright eyes.

I get my phone out – time to share a moment. Hey all! As you can see, I'm here, it's me, *finalement* in Paris. This bridge is called the Petit Pont right next to Notre-Dame. What do you think of my scarf?! *Tres chic n'est ce-pas?* SEND.

My heart feels kind of achy - a disconcerting swell of ambiguous feelings. There's a light breeze but you wouldn't call it a breeze, it's a waft. It seems to be carried by the river. What does it smell like? What would Proust say? Old wet stone, river weed and a touch of marine diesel? No matter, cos the air comes alive just for me, funnelling under the bridges and rippling over the waves. I let it cool my neck, pushing up my hair. Get those Hepburn shades on, a hair flick, a wry smile, is that the Louvre in the background? Look at you, Little Miss Independent. Click, send to Maisy, Diane, Cal, Charlie, who else? Send to Luke? Tempting – check me out huh? I'm doing just fine, so suck it up. No, cheap shot. Don't send to Luke.

They're waving from the boat as they slide right under where I stand, happy couples, tourists, so many cameras and phones. Does anyone come here and just look at stuff with their eyes anymore? What do they take home from Paris? Three thousand image files to gather dust on a digital cloud? But I'm here, I'm looking at it straight, unfiltered. It's Paris, these big white clouds framing the towers of Notre-Dame, this precious stone bridge, and buzzing along the embankment near me is a cool guy riding a funky scooter-bike and he's wearing a black business suit, aviator shades and a retro helmet. Maybe he's going to a meeting at a creative agency, he's going to jump off his bike and stride into the board-room, taking off his shades, straightening his tie; 'Salut, Salut', purposeful handshakes all round.

Thinking about men, again. Motorbike guy is not for me. Monsieur Le Scarf is more my type. I'm smiling at the clouds now. It was charming, our little conversation. His eyes were kind, with a hint of naughtiness. When did anyone last charm me? A *frisson* is what I felt, a little French word that fluttered inside me and stirred the memory of desire. Admit it. How thrilling it would be to meet someone here, in Paris, to have a little affair of the heart, an *amour*. Not to seek it out but just to be open to the possibility. That someone else might take control and all I need to do is to react, all decisions made, all responsibility assumed.

Did I always have these conversations with myself? Of course, of course. I just never noticed before. I suppose I was too busy ticking things off my list. Looking back, all these predictable stages in my life. And now I'm old enough to just list them right off like the chapter headings of a book. It goes something like:

    High school

    First dates

    Columbia

    English and French Lit

    Lacrosse

    Two serious relationships

    Luke

    First jobs

    An unnecessarily big wedding

    Moving to LA

    Promotions

    Cal, then Charlie

    Junior soccer

    Lots of baking

    Vacations in the Caribbean

    Less conversation

    Less sex

Less love

Less Luke

Less life?

I don't want those California days anymore, the endless smoggy hazy blue. I want more contrast. I like this dappled life, the *promise* of sunshine, the towering white clouds underlined with grey, seem more real, or is it just a better metaphor? The clouds move west over Paris and the sun pours out a molten wave of golden light that sweeps across the quayside, turns the river into quicksilver – this is how Seurat must have seen it. Sparkling atoms, colour saturated.

This change of light, this impressionist moment. I want to cherish it, to add it to the myriad other moments. Let me focus on it, let me be in the now. But something is niggling. It's like the telling of a dream, you know when you have it in your head as clear as a movie scene and then it just unravels in the telling. Where did it go, why can't I find the words? What is it with me? I'm like that princess in the story, you know, the one about the pea and the pile of mattresses and however comfortable she gets on all those mattresses she can still feel that damned pea. I'm in this sumptuous scene, but there's a little pea rattling in my head. It's been two months since I came off the meds. I didn't want to see Paris in muted tones. I need edges. If it has to be gritty and sharp

I'll take it, not like before. Citalopram got me through the worst times. It dulls the pain. I coped. The ugly accusations from his divorce lawyers. The kids' recriminations. What did we say to them: 'You're old enough to understand. You're such great kids, we know you will be OK. We just need to live our own lives now'. So trite, it's embarrassing. You rationalise everything but deep down I know they are still hurting, especially Cal.

On one stall, amongst the paperbacks, the copies of Le Petit Journal and the antique maps I find a tray of vintage postcards. One black and white card catches my eye. A lady in a full length black skirt, Victorian era, is standing at one of the bouquiniste stalls peering intently at the display. Perched on her head is a dainty straw hat like a boater – it probably has coloured ribbons or pattern, but we can't tell. She's carrying a strong looking leather handbag, big enough for a book or two. Behind her, several men, all wearing bowler hats, are reading or just strolling by. One is close to her and leans confidently against the stand - he must be the bouquiniste. Curiously, he is looking at her feet or at the hem of her dress. Maybe he was thinking: 'Is she a buyer or a time-waster?' Or perhaps he was staring furtively at her impressive bosom before the photographer was ready to press the shutter and then he quickly dropped his eyes to the ground beneath her at the crucial moment?

This postcard is . . . what? Ephemera? It is nothing, yet, it tells a story. It is, it was, a moment perhaps with some minor intrigue, laden with delicate possibilities. Here are the trees on the quai above her head, there is the wooden box with its padlocks, just as it is today. There's a glimpse of the Seine and on the far side you can see the grey rooftops of the Île de la Cité. She's got her eye on a volume. But what is it? Or is she aware of the bouquiniste's glance and she has deliberately averted her gaze? She will think 'these book-sellers are scruffy bohemians and how disarming that he should leer at me'. She is a teacher, she has some standing. In a tall-ceilinged class room smelling of bees-wax floor polish her pupils await their next lesson, but still she idles at the stall. She can't resist a volume of Molière's École des Femmes. A few francs are spared from her purse, the volume disappears into her capacious leather bag and the bouquiniste tips his hat, with a little too much of a flourish, she feels. Perhaps she will be reprimanded for being late for her class? They will say 'Madame So and So, this is the third time we have spoken of this matter, it is really too unconscionable!' And it will be Molière's fault. And will she return to the scene of the crime, for a surreptitious second appraisal of the bouquiniste?

Or maybe it was a work by Proust, not Moliere? But that seems unlikely. I don't think Proust was born then, or perhaps he was just born, so his first memories were forming unknowingly before his new-seeing eyes – the colours and scents and sounds of new life. Do babies even know what to think? Are they just in a purity of being?

You need to get away they said. Diane urging me on a literary tour: 'Remember how you were such a book-worm? They have all these European tours for people just like you'. And Maisy, brash as ever: 'Get yourself to Paris girl, go drink too much and let some suave Frenchman take you to bed! You deserve nothing less!' And even the kids, ok a little reluctant at first, but eventually they got bored with my dreams and it was 'For God's sake Mom just go!'

What is it I'm looking for? What is this Paris that will transform me? It is overwhelming. These Monets and Manets, these grand palaces, a self-conscious pause for a café creme at Les Deux Magots, a stroll along the left bank boulevards and a day among the lanes and stairways of Montmartre in search of the ghosts of famous writers and painters. And all I seem to find is a tedious version of me. My threadbare personal history, so predictable and modest it fits on a shopping list, seems to shadow me as I visit these places of pilgrimage. I feel like a jaded tour guide who can't shake off a rag tag trail of unwanted clients.

I must get a grip. Start walking again. Away from the bridge. Back to the apartment? Airbnb came up trumps, even though Jules the owner turned out to be in London. The place is kind of fusty, but he has an incredible library of books, that little balcony is a gem, and the views! I could kick off these heels and take a book outside and just chill. Comforting. But instead I'm heading back to the bouquinistes. Why go back? Because it's the opposite to what my head says I should do? It feels kind of tough and brave anyway. Time to let things go. Admit painfully that, it is, to be completely honest, a pretty slim effort so far, the story of my life. More of a short story than a book. It starts conventionally, with some promise and early pace, but then it becomes a bit stodgy, the prose is unexciting, the plot predictable, and the end? Who knows? But if you happened upon it by chance on a stall here in Paris, well, would you be drawn to open it? Would you read it with curiosity or even with sympathy? Who will care for such unfinished prose one spring day in a hundred years' time? It will probably sit snug in alongside the cheaper paperbacks, with their lurid covers promising romance and adventure, until eventually the pages will become faded and begin to tear away. But until then, consider the wider company it will keep on this book-lined quay-side! Latin poets, Ecclesiastical treatises, vintage celebrity magazines, comic book superheroes, penny romances, old newspapers reporting victories and defeats on long grubbed up battlefields, leather bound volumes of Descartes, Stein, Pound, Zola, Baudelaire. All these authors, all these scribblers, all dead. Au revoir petit livre!

Message to Diane, doyenne of the reading group: 'Starting a new chapter!', with a selfie of me in front of the bouquinistes. SEND. She will understand.

I walk away, anywhere. Across the avenue into the flower market. Heady scent of hyacinths, branches of lilac arching over the stalls and the reflections of clouds in the silvery puddles of discarded flower water. I buy some pink tulips for my kitchen table. Outside the market there's a pavement café with a chalkboard and ironwork tables. At one of the tables I notice Monsieur Le Scarf. With one hand he slowly stirs a coffee and with the other he is holding open a paperback which he reads intently.

## About the author

Guy Hibbert is an award-winning journalist and author who has lived in and travelled extensively across France during the past twenty years. He is Editor in Chief of France Today magazine and writes regular articles about French culture, history and art de vivre.

He is currently working on a novel set in Rome as well as a new volume of short stories set in France. He divides his time between Bath, England and the south of France.

If you have enjoyed these stories, please tell your friends and take a moment to write a review on Amazon or Goodreads. Thank you.

www.guyhibbert.com

# The Château of Illusions

The beautiful white limestone Château of Lusone, designed and built by the Picards, once proud Cognac producers, has fallen into the hands of the aristocratic Duplessis family. The mysteries of the château are the poignant backdrop to an unfolding story of two families, each new generation becoming entwined in a web of intrigue, love, revenge and redemption.

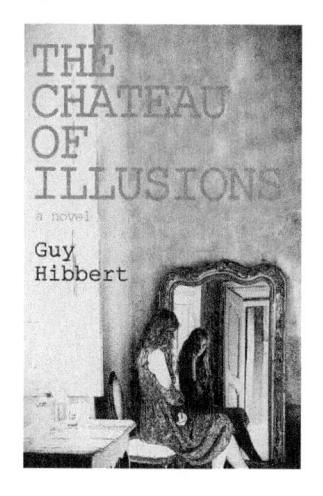

The Château of Illusions moves from south west France to Paris, London and back to France again, telling the story of Thérèse Picard and her relationships with the two Duplessis brothers, Roland and François. From blissful pre-war summers to heartache and heroism during World War 2, her journey from wilful youth to brave adult is swift and painful. As the saga sweeps forward through the extravagant 1960s and into the 1980s an extraordinary work of art is discovered, and hidden secrets revealed. With the 40th anniversary of VE Day approaching, a series of dramatic revelations lead to unforeseen twists of fate for both families.

Guy Hibbert has conjured up an epic page turner full of vivid detail, lively and intriguing characters and a reluctant heroine who endures her loves and losses with determination and courage.